CHARLES

Darkness #8

K.F. BREENE

Copyright © 2015 by K.F. Breene

All rights reserved. The people, places and situations contained in this ebook are figments of the author's imagination and in no way reflect real or true events.

❦ Created with Vellum

SYNOPSIS

Charles is a guy that likes to play the field. He's highly sought after in the Mansion, both for his prowess, and his position. He's content to stay the playboy for life, too, steeped in the culture in which he was raised.

That is, until he finds himself on a mission with Ann, trying to figure out why shifters are mysteriously going missing. Suddenly things that were so clear cut, get muddled.

When Ann succumbs to the danger that is plaguing her kind, all bets are off.

CHAPTER ONE

Charles separated himself from the tangle of limbs and staggered away from the bed. He looked down at himself before trying to wipe off his chest in heavy pats. Glitter sparkled on his pecs and abs like a disco ball.

This is what it had come to. Glitter. How he thought glitter had been a good idea, the Gods only knew.

He snatched up his clothes and headed for the door. The girls on the bed didn't even shift. They wouldn't notice his absence until the evening, and wouldn't even care that he was gone when they did.

Charles made his way through the mostly empty Mansion as daylight wrestled with the heavy curtains, some sneaking through to splash the walls and floor. Only a few humans wandered through the corridors, keeping watch. All Paulie's hires, the humans were thick, robust dudes with guns, swords, and shifty eyes. Many had prison tats, very few could do magic, and all would take an axe to an intruder's head just to spice up their weapon choice. Given that they weren't the most violent in the Mansion—Jonas probably still held that title—they fit in just fine. Real nice guys when a male got to know them, actually.

Charles let himself into his room and heaved a tired sigh. His dick hurt.

He looked down at the tired soldier, resting peacefully among meticulous man-scaping.

What had his world come to when sex became mundane? He'd screwed his way through the Mansion these last couple weeks trying to find the joy he had once held for constant sex. A single partner wasn't really doing it for him, so he'd tried two and three girls at a time. That was just a lot of work, so he'd tried a guy, which had been uncomfortable at best.

Lately, he'd let girls deck him in chocolate, or glitter, and last night, he'd almost said yes to wearing an animal suit.

An animal suit.

Charles dropped his clothes and put his phone on the nightstand.

"Something's gone very wrong when you're thinking about roaring like a lion in a leotard just to get off." His voice sounded unnaturally loud in the silence.

He jumped in the shower before sliding into bed, noticing a few sparkles still glimmering on his chest. He'd never get that shit off.

No more glitter.

As his body started to relax, he took a moment to go over the things he was thankful for in life, and as always, lingered on the children, even though none of them were his. Jonas' little girl had just started walking, teetering around with a beautiful little face just like Emmy. She was the sweetest thing Charles had ever seen, loving cuddles and being held tightly. She offset Sasha's two villains, who were constantly getting into mischief, working together to create more havoc than any two kids should. Paulie's little boy was more of a watcher, studying the room before getting a wild urge to sprint through, often barreling into things without fear.

Charles smiled as his heart warmed, wishing he'd gone to Sasha and the Boss' house tonight. He was in a good spot as the beloved uncle, getting all the love and smiles without the responsibility, but he'd be lying if he said he didn't miss them when he was away. When he left, it was to his own room and solitude.

Maybe he just needed new partners. A vacation to another territory with all new females might drum up his desire again.

He settled deep into his pillows, letting the tiredness overcome him.

Whatever he needed, it definitely wasn't glitter. He'd have to try and scrub off the rest of it before he saw Jonas or Paulie or he'd never hear the end of it.

∼

"Is that glitter?" Jonas prodded Charles' neck with a heavy finger.

Charles couldn't help a gag from where the poke landed. "Bro, not cool. You can't go around trying to choke people with that hammy finger."

"I can if they're trying to impersonate a thirteen year old girl. You've got glitter on your neck."

Charles, Jonas, and Paulie walked out the back door of the Mansion, making their way to the area where the Watch was going through some training exercises.

"Just trying to please the ladies, bro," Charles said as they neared. He noticed a couple of the larger humans who'd recently come to the Mansion to be trained in magic. They both had red-level power, but could probably push up a level with training. What's more, they had martial arts training. Good additions, all of them.

Paulie snorted. "Pleasing a chick for the night is nothing. Half the time they don't say nothin' when you fail—they expect it. Pleasing a chick you have to live with..." Paulie shook his head. "Mine stopped pretending to come. But Christ—chicks are a lotta work. Is it God's joke that they are so hard to get off? She wants it every day—I don't got it in me, man. Too much work. Rather just take a hand to it half the time—quick and easy."

Jonas sniffed. "It takes a real male to please his female. It takes a halfwit to parade around in glitter with a swinging dick, and a useless male to bitch about getting it every day."

"Useless, huh? Talk to me when you get it every day again. You've got a six-month old—your lady isn't *trying* to deal with you," Paulie growled. "But I got some time—why don't I beat the shit outta you right quick? Let's see about *useless*."

Jonas turned toward Paulie. His muscles flexed up and down his thick frame, hearing the challenge and ready to answer. Paulie stared back, fire fueling his eyes.

Charles rolled his eyes as Mick, one of the strategists who worked with Jameson, strode toward them. He hoped the nerd wanted to talk to Jonas or Paulie rather than to him. "We all know you're not going to fight until the more advanced Watch trains later tonight. Like you do every night," he said. "What's the point in staring at each other? It's annoying."

"The human is trying to get his courage up," Jonas said, turning back to face the training.

"Must suck to admit to people you got beat the fuck up by a human..." Paulie rasped as he turned back to the training too.

Paulie had really come into his own in the last year or so. He'd made great strides with his magic and advanced dramatically with his hand-to-hand combat. In his fights with Jonas, he now won as often as he lost, which was quite an achievement.

"He's used to it," Charles said as he watched the swordwork of the humans. "Sasha blasts him with magic on a regular basis."

"Not as much as you," Jonas retaliated.

"Charles, sir..." Charles sighed and turned to Mick, too stiff and proper by half. The night was off to a rocky start. "The Boss requests your presence in the Purple Library."

"Why didn't you bring a formal invite?" Charles asked sarcastically as he glanced at Jonas. Jonas gave him a nod, acknowledging his leaving.

"I didn't realize you could read, sir. I will in future." Mick led the way with small steps.

"Funny guy. How funny will you look hanging from your ankles, I wonder?"

"Not as funny as walking around with glitter on my arms, I would imagine."

That was the problem with smart guys—they weren't easy to pick on.

Mick stopped at the side of the doorway to the Purple Library and gestured Charles ahead of him. Charles walked in to find the Boss sitting in the far corner. In the chair beside him lounged Tim, the alpha of the shifters. His big, brown eyes matched the color of the giant Kodiak bear he turned into. Only six feet tall as a human, Tim was stocky and coordinated, but easily taken in a fight. It was that bear form, though, that gave a male the shivers. That beast was a giant slab of muscle, violence, and death, lumbering around a battlefield with razor sharp claws and a vicious growl.

A few other shifters loitered around the edges of the room, eyes alert but bodies relaxed. Ann leaned against the far wall with a shock of blue hair, her cupid's mouth turned up into the easy smile she was known for. She gave Charles a wink in welcome as he caught her gaze.

The annoying brainiac, Mick, left Charles to join Jameson on the far side of the room.

One person was missing. "Where's Sasha?"

The Boss looked up at him. That dark-eyed stare, filled with power and authority, was enough to make Charles' spine tingle in warning.

"Here." Sasha strolled into the room with a swollen belly and a surly expression. "Stefan still insists on weekly checkups by both a human doctor and a clan doctor. I'm barely six months pregnant—I'm not that fragile."

Charles felt a surge of protectiveness—a natural response to a female carrying a child for their kind. The Boss, who must've felt ten times the protectiveness since it was his child, stood and turned all of his focus toward her. He took her hand and led her to a cushioned seat next to him before resettling, leaving his hand on the arm of her chair protectively.

Charles grabbed the chair facing them and turned it around so he could sit next to her, too.

"I'm not in a touchy-feely-kind of mood, Charles," Sasha warned.

Undeterred, he waited until Sasha was distracted with the Boss' presence before sneaking his hand onto her belly. He loved feeling the baby move. It was a trip.

A bolt of electricity sizzled up his arm and zinged into his body. All his muscles tensed and his jaw clenched shut with pain. "Damn it, Sasha. You have to share!"

"Get your own woman to knock up," she retorted.

"And be tied to a nutcase like you?"

"Charles." The Boss' deep voice claimed Charles' focus. Just barely. "Tim is having a problem with shifters going missing in the Headland Foothills."

"We've sent in two teams," Tim said, moving in his seat to turn his shoulders toward Charles. "The first was a few months back. We still haven't heard anything. The second went in two weeks ago tomorrow. Same as before—phones went off the grid, as did GPS trackers. We haven't heard a word."

Charles slid his hand onto Sasha's chair arm, sneaking it closer so he could move it to her stomach when she wasn't paying attention. He turned his focus to Tim, thinking over what was said. Who said males couldn't multitask?

"What kind of people are you sending in?" Charles asked. "And why did you send anyone in the first place? What tipped you off?"

"We have occasional patrols in mountain areas for shifters who are going through the change, or have gone through it and are staying away from humans. We try to find these people and incorporate them into our faction. The patrol went missing, which happens occasionally—some of the wild ones are powerful and dangerous. I then sent in a group of ten preparing for a hostile response. Those ten were highly trained, experienced, and ruthless. They are always prepared for the worst, and wouldn't engage if they were outnumbered. Their last check-in was normal. They'd seen no sign of foul-play. Two hours later, their tracking devices vanished. We haven't heard anything from them since."

Charles calmly extended his hand to Sasha's belly as his gaze switched to the Boss. "That's way beyond our territory—have you heard anything from the neighboring clan?"

The Boss glanced at Jameson, who had a map laid out on a table. "I called. They haven't had any problems."

"*Any* problems?" Charles asked.

"Anything out of the ordinary. Their scuffles for territory with the neighboring clan don't extend into the mountains."

"Any reason they wouldn't fill you in if they did have problems?" Tim asked the Boss.

The Boss shook his head. "They're trying to stay in my good graces. Since I took over the territory to the north, they've been happy to work with me."

The clan leader to the north had been a real dick. After killing Andris, the Boss had naturally expanded to take over the unoccupied territory. It was his right, after all. He and Sasha were the ones who had taken out Andris, so by rule, Andris' territory should go to the winning party. Logic.

The weakling leader from the north had seen an opportunity, though, and tried to take it for himself. Charles had been there when the Boss attempted to handle the dispute diplomatically. The leader had challenged.

Now he was dead.

It didn't pay to underestimate the Boss, especially with Sasha at his back.

"So you're requesting aid?" Charles affirmed.

Tim nodded once.

"But you're not requesting aid from the clan in that area because you're not on great terms with them?" Charles verified.

"Amazing powers of information recall, Charles," Sasha said in a dry voice. "That's only been the case... I don't know... for*ever*."

Charles stopped the retort as it was about to leave his mouth. If he gave her sass, she'd blast his hand and probably send him reeling across the room.

"How many of the Watch are you requesting?" Charles asked.

"One. For now." Tim's eyes hardened. "We're blind in that area. I don't want to send any more people than we have to until we know what we're up against. I was hoping your magic, or your ability to influence humans, might make the difference. I'll send one of mine with you. All we need is reconnaissance and a safe return. That's it."

Charles took his hand from Sasha and leaned forward, looking at the Boss. "And you've elected me." It wasn't a question.

"Tim is sending Ann," the Boss said. Ann shifted in the corner. "You work best with her. I realize Paulie is better with magic than you are, and he and she get along, but he is half-human and lacks pheromones. You're the next best bet."

"What else do we know?" Charles glanced at Jameson.

On cue, Jameson stepped forward. "Satellites aren't covering that area, so we have no idea what could be up there. As Tim's technology is cutting out, I have a feeling it is something with advanced facilities. That smacks of government forces or highly funded private organizations." Jameson's gaze hit Tim. "I've not heard of any humans going missing in that area. The newspapers would jump on that story. There have been a few new clips in the tabloids about werewolves. Tabloids cash in on popular rumor, which means people are talking. I wouldn't be surprised if the genetic mutation that allows humans to shift into animals has been suspected. This situation is probably shifter-specific."

"We're thinking the same thing," Tim said in something close to a growl. "This happens every so often, and has throughout history, but technology is so advanced now that all it takes is a little bit of bloodwork and a curious lab technician."

"A lab?" Charles' words came out a whisper. He looked at Ann, standing stiffly in the corner. This wasn't a situation where she might be killed in action. If she was caught, and it was a lab with its sights on shifters, she'd be taken and experimented on. That was a fate worse than death. She didn't need to be anywhere near that.

"I don't need her. I can go on my own," he said.

Everyone in the room stared at him for a moment. Ann stepped forward with a scowl. "If there are traps, they'll be triggered by a shifter, not a big goon with a huge ego. You might never find out how they're capturing our people."

"If you get caught, I'll have to concentrate on rescuing you instead of gaining information," Charles fired back.

"Charles, this is Tim's operation," the Boss interjected. "You'll be accompanying Ann, as well as taking your cues from her. She is lead on this."

"Why her?" Charles blurted despite himself. "What if she's caught?"

"She volunteered," Tim said in an even voice.

"And you're just going to let her go?"

"Are you saying I can't do my job?" Ann asked savagely, taking another step forward.

Charles glared at her, unexplainable anger welling up and taking over. "I'm saying that he is accountable for you as both your alpha and your boyfriend. When you're acting like an idiot, he needs to help you tone it down."

"Charles, Ann is going to kick your ass if you don't shut up," Sasha warned.

"You're excused, Charles," the Boss said in a flat tone. "You will accompany whoever Tim decides to send. Now get out."

The command had Charles standing against his will, the Boss' dominating tone overriding his complaints, but he gave Ann a long look before shaking his head. "You're going to make me play the hero, and then I'm going to hold it over you for the rest of your life. Think that through."

Ann scoffed. "Just because you wear a cape around the Mansion to wow the ladies doesn't mean you're a hero. And nice glitter, dumbass."

"And don't forget about tomorrow," Sasha called as he was leaving the room. "Party at our house."

Charles tossed a wave behind him saying he heard Sasha as he left the library. This mission was a bad idea. Everything in him said *danger,* and not for himself. Ann was capable, he wasn't denying that, but she was also headstrong and fearless. She'd rush into danger to keep others out of harm's way, possibly getting herself caught in the process.

With his night suddenly down the crap-chute he made his way back out to the training. It was time to fight Jonas or Paulie. He needed to burn off some aggression.

CHAPTER TWO

The next evening, Ann blinked her eyes open and spread out a hand to the other side of her bed.

Empty.

She heaved a sigh and rolled onto her back, hearing the vibration of her phone on her desk across the room. Groaning, she swung her feet to the edge of the bed and let gravity help her feet find the floor. She walked stiffly to the desk, muscles sore from the intense workouts she'd been doing to keep her mind occupied.

Sasha's name scrolled across the face of the phone, her smiling mug mocking the time.

"Did you notice the time before you called?" Ann asked by way of greeting, staggering back to her bed. She fell into the warmth of her blankets.

"Your alarm is going to go off in a few minutes. I'm helping you wake up. You're welcome."

Ann eyed the alarm clock on the nightstand. Five o'clock in the evening. Shifters didn't keep the hours the Boss' people did, shifters not having the same predisposition for the night, but Ann had volunteered for night duty to keep similar hours to Sasha. After getting used to it, now it had become second nature.

Unless she didn't get a lot of sleep during the day. Which had been the case lately.

"How are things?" Sasha asked quietly.

Ann let her gaze fall to the side, not having to ask what Sasha meant. "Lonely. I can't get used to waking up alone."

"Do you miss him?"

Ann curled onto her side, away from the empty place so recently filled with a warm body and loving embrace. "I miss the idea of him. I miss someone constant in my life."

"I talked to him."

Ann's breath caught. It had been a week since Tim had ended their relationship. He was a good man, loving and thoughtful. She hadn't seen the breakup coming.

"I don't think I want to know what he said," Ann said quietly.

"He loves you. You know that. But he also knows you don't love him. You have your sights set on someone else. Guys can tell. You can't blame him for setting you free."

Ann wiped away a tear. "He broke it off, but he's still making it my fault…"

"Guys are tricky."

Ann laughed as her alarm started blaring. She tapped the 'off' button and went back to her fetal position. "He was right —I didn't love him. I tried, though. I did try, Sasha. He's a great catch."

"I know."

"I enjoyed being with him."

"Or… do you just hate being alone…?"

Ann sat up, a deep ache in the middle of her body for things she knew she could never have. She sighed and glanced toward the window, covered in heavy drapes. Heaving herself off the bed she walked across the room and pulled back the curtains. Outside the dwindling sunlight stretched the shadows of the trees across the ground.

She had to admit that Tim had been right—she did love someone else. She couldn't help it. The more she was around this other guy, the stronger her feelings became wrapped around him. She thought about him constantly—his funny jokes, his dense responses, his deep and soulful personality when he allowed himself the freedom to express himself honestly.

She tried desperately to block out those feelings. It wasn't meant to be. The one she wanted was from a different world, living by a different set of rules. The things she wanted would clip his wings, and she knew it. She couldn't force that on him.

Ann leaned against the wall. "This sucks. How did you find Mr. Monogamy?"

"The only time in my life I got lucky, I think. You shouldn't dwell on it, though. Tim's great, but he wasn't the one. There is someone else out there for you."

"Yeah."

"In the meantime, get laid. It helps. Seriously."

Ann huffed out a laugh and crossed to her closet. "Is my time to feel sorry for myself over already?"

"Well, since you're the reason for the breakup... yeah." Sasha's tone was light and playful, with a deep well of support infusing her words.

"I'm ready, though, Sasha," Ann admitted, taking out the sweats she'd wear to the perimeter. After that, she'd stash them and change into her animal form. "When you first got pregnant with the twins, I didn't think I ever wanted a husband or kids. I was happy on my own. But now... I'm ready. I want a version of what you have. Only, you know, one kid at a time."

"At least I'm only having one this time. So much easier."

Sasha sighed. "But I hear ya. And he's out there. Just look for Mr. Right Now for a while, and eventually the Now part will just drop away."

"Got any leads on guys that are great in bed?"

"There you go! Now you're talking. And yeah, there'll be a few hotties at the party tonight. Go for someone from the Mansion, they have more experience—babe, I'm not talking about people *I* find attractive," Sasha's voice drifted away from the phone. She must've been talking to Stefan. "I am solely thinking of Ann here..."

Ann laughed as a deep rumble sounded in the background, Stefan's protective instincts in overdrive since Sasha had fallen pregnant. Once Ann would've thought that highly restrictive, but knowing why he did it, and how Sasha reveled in it when pregnant, Ann couldn't help the tiny fingers of envy.

"I hate you." It had to be said.

Sasha scoffed. "He's not going to let me out of his sight at the party. I'm going to have a big, dominating presence behind me at all times."

"You do, anyway."

"Yes, but this time he'll be scaring all male guests. Yes, Stefan—you know you're going to kill the party..."

Ann laughed and sat next to her clothes on the bed. The deep rumble sounded in the background again. Sasha threw out another scoff, but a kiss sounded away from the phone.

"Are you done?" Ann asked in faux-impatience.

"Yeah, sorry. Anyway, come looking fabulous. Make-up, dress—the works. It'll make you feel more desirable. And Tim can't make it tonight, so it's not like you'd be rubbing salt in his wounds or anything. We have plenty of beds for you to get your freak on."

"You are advocating slutty behavior."

"Um, *yes*. Yes I am. You're old enough to enjoy sex without someone calling you names. So enjoy it. With someone good at it."

"Got it. Gotta go, though. I'm on perimeter duty tonight."

"Kay. Bye."

Before Sasha hung up, Ann heard, "Stefan, come back in here. I'm horn—"

Shaking her head, she pulled on her clothes for the evening. Hopefully someone would try to get into the shifter compound. She could really do with some violence.

In the small hours of the morning, after her duty was finished, Ann showed up at Sasha's huge house on the edge of the city. She wore a tight red dress with a slit in the side running up, all the way to her upper thigh. The neckline plunged down in a low vee, showing off her braless breasts. She'd dyed her hair jet black, a color that worked well with the tone of her skin, and done her make-up.

She looked hot.

Well... at least as hot as she was capable of looking, which was good enough.

She let herself into the brightly lit house, immediately assaulted with the thrum of bass. Laughter and chatter drifted to the entryway, the party already going strong.

With a case of butterflies from entering a party on her own for the first time in nearly a year, she made her way through the foyer and into the living room. A large room opened up with a few kids tussling in the middle of the open space, hanging off of a large, broad back. The man on the ground roared as he straightened up, the kids squealing with glee as he lifted into the air while they hung on for dear life.

Charles' striking face came into view, red with exertion

and smiling. He held his arms to the sides, his huge muscles popping out all over his frame. "You cannot take down the mountain!"

Sabrina, one of Sasha's twins, giggled in delight as she ran in front of him. Her brother still hung onto one of Charles' arms while Paulie's son held onto the other.

"I save you!" Sabrina declared with an evil grin. She brought her foot back and let fly, giving Charles a sound kick to the groin.

"Oh my—" Charles cut off and curled up with a wheeze, dropping the boys to the carpet and rolling into the fetal position. "Foul play! Foul play!"

"Sabrina!" Sasha hollered from the side of the room, sitting on the couch with Stefan right beside her. Stefan had a huge smile on his face. "What did I say about kicking Charles there?"

Sabrina looked down at the ground. She clasped her three-year-old hands in front of her. "Not to."

"Say you're sorry," Sasha commanded as she elbowed Stefan. "It's not funny."

"It's very funny. She's tough." Stefan's smile dwindled in the face of Sasha's anger, but his dark eyes twinkled in mirth as he watched Charles writhing on the floor.

"Sowy Chawles," Sabrina said with sad eyes and a pout. She was a little shit-disturber, but she hated getting in trouble. Telling her she was a bad girl was as bad to her as a spanking.

"Aw, it's okay," Charles said as he reached for her and reeled her into a hug.

Savion, her twin brother, didn't have the same reservations. With a war-cry, he threw himself onto Charles and started pounding on his back.

"No! No!" Charles groaned.

"Savion!" Sasha shouted. "Stefan, will you do something?"

Laughing, Stefan got up from the couch and scooped up the boys. "C'mon you guys, it's time to go play in your playroom."

"Wait for me, daddy!" Sabrina wiggled out from Charles' grasp and tore off after Stefan.

"Ow." Charles rolled to his back. His large arms flopped out to the sides as his chest heaved. "They get more violent every time I see them. They're teaching Todd bad things, Paulie."

Paulie stood off to the side with a beer and his achingly beautiful wife, Selene. He grinned down at Charles. "Survival. He's in a violent group of people—I wouldn't want him turning out like you."

Charles sat up with a wince. "Bro, you'd be so lucky."

Ann walked farther into the room, heading for Sasha, when people started noticing her presence. The frustration of dealing with her kids melted off Sasha's face as she smiled up at Ann. She grunted as she pushed herself off the couch.

"Look at you, Ann!" Sasha exclaimed, wrapping Ann in a hug.

"Hot mama!" Selene came over with warm smile, trailed by Paulie. Ann hugged them both before glancing at Charles.

Charles' eyes were wide and his mouth had fallen open, his gaze slowly drifting down her body. He got to his feet slowly, his hand cupping his crotch. "I've had practice with guys, Ann. Think Tim would be into a three-way? Because you are sex on a stick and I need to eat you."

"Jaysus!" Sasha slapped him. "Way overboard. *Way!*"

"What? Eat, as in, lick her—"

"We get it!" Sasha cut him off with wide eyes. "Good God, Charles. This is a family establishment."

Selene started laughing. "He gets away with anything in the Mansion. All the girls line up for his time. The more crude, the more they love him."

"We aren't in the Mansion, man," Paulie cut in, clapping Charles on the back. His eyes crinkled at the corners, obviously finding Charles' comments funny. "You gotta pull that back. Subtly."

A grin tweaked Charles full lips. His eyes softened. "You look beautiful, Ann. I hope Tim appreciates what he has."

Selene and Sasha's mouths both rounded. Paulie started laughing.

"When did the Casanova show up?" Selene asked as she looked at Charles with raised eyebrows.

"What?" Charles looked between the two flabbergasted women. "Girls like that sort of thing. They want you to notice when they look pretty. I've seen all the romance movies—seriously, women love that shit! Just because you two are jaded doesn't mean everyone is."

Paulie laughed harder.

"One hundred and one ways to get into her pants, huh, Charles?" Sasha said with a grin.

"Do you want a drink, Ann?" Selene asked as she shook her head.

"Wine, please," Ann said, hoping her red face didn't show through her make-up as warmth rose through her core. She obviously wouldn't admit it now, but she knew Charles was being genuine. He really did think she looked pretty—otherwise he'd ask why she looked like a garbage bin, or some other horrendous thing. He had a large streak of honesty she loved, especially because when he paid a compliment he meant it.

Charles turned serious. "Where's Tim, anyway? I wanted to talk to him about the mission tomorrow."

"She broke up with him, Charles. Drop it, would ya?" Sasha said out of the corner of her mouth as she stepped toward Ann.

"Wait… what?" Charles asked as Sasha took Ann's upper

arm and steered her toward the back of the house. "Is that a green light for me?"

"No," Sasha shot back at him. "Go away."

"But Sasha, she might need a rebound. I am excellent at rebound situations. I take great pride in making women scream. And I almost got all the glitter off, so I'm manly again."

"You have a long way to go to be manly. Go away!" Sasha shooed him as she directed Ann through an archway and into the den. Men and women chatted in groups, all from the Mansion, and all beautiful.

"Why so quiet?" Sasha asked as they stepped up next to the small bar in the corner. Selene had gotten there first. She passed Ann a glass of wine.

"Just taking it all in. I haven't been this dressed up in... forever." Ann took a sip and let her gaze travel the hot men, noticing more than a few glance her way.

"Well, drink up. You're just traveling tomorrow, right? You can have a hangover and post-coital buzz." Sasha looked up as Stefan came into the room, pulling eyes to him like the sun pulled planets. He honed in on Sasha, sparing no one else a glance.

"Out of curiosity, why did you volunteer for that job?" Selene asked as Stefan slid his hand around Sasha's back and pulled her in close to his body. His gaze hit Ann.

"Hey Stefan," Ann said before answering Selene, "Why not?"

"Because you could get captured and experimented on, for a start." Jonas walked up with an empty beer bottle. He nodded to the bartender, then Stefan, before putting his bottle on the bar for the bartender to whisk away.

"Or I could save the day." Ann took another sip of her drink, trying to ignore the raging butterflies in her belly.

"Does it have anything to do with breaking up with that mongrel?" Jonas asked, his hard eyes analyzing Ann.

"Such sweet words you speak, Jonas," she answered in a dry voice.

He snorted and shifted, looking out over the room. If Stefan drew eyes, Jonas pushed them away. Suddenly everyone had something else of great importance to focus on, and that thing was not the intense guy looking at them like they were terrorists.

"And no, it doesn't." Ann noticed Selene and Sasha both look down at their drinks. "Okay, maybe a little."

Jonas nodded. "The child will have your back. He's not as dumb as he looks. Most of the time."

"Just keep your eyes peeled," Stefan said as he stared at her. "Let Charles lead with magic. I almost wonder if we should send Paulie, too."

"That might make Tim want to send another mongrel." Jonas took a sip of his beer. "Too big a party would be noticed."

"Paulie is also trigger-happy," Selene said. "He has great instincts, but if something seems off, he'll kill first and report after. He's hasty. He's got the wrong skill set for this."

"Can we change the subject?" Ann finished her glass of wine, handing it to Sasha who looked at the empty glass in longing before passing it behind her to get refilled.

"Parties aren't nearly as much fun when I'm not drinking." Sasha grimaced at her water.

"So, see anyone you like?" Selene asked, waggling her eyebrows. She jerked her head out toward the men in the room. "Just point him out and I'll give you the skinny."

Ann sighed and allowed Selene to lead her away from the guys. She might as well start the rebound hunt now.

Five hours and several glasses of wine later, Ann found herself stumbling outside for some air and a breather. Her head buzzed with alcohol and her lady parts buzzed with desire. She had guys doting on her constantly, excited with the rare prospect of getting to try a shifter in bed. She was the exotic party favor.

Strangely, in the mood she was in, she was totally okay with that. All she had to do was point at the person she wanted, and she would get him. Or them. In true Mansion fashion, they were okay with sharing.

She closed the sliding glass door behind her. She needed a break.

A giggle sounded off to her right, followed by a masculine hum. Ann veered to the left, feeling the cool breeze against her fevered skin. She lifted her hair off the nape of her neck and leaned against the wall of the house as her gaze traveled the shimmering swimming pool.

"Ann?"

Ann glanced to where a man and a woman stood in the faint light of dawn. The drop-dead gorgeous woman gave a whine of disapproval as Charles stepped forward. The light splashed across his handsome features, illuminating his smoky, grey eyes. Without saying anything to the woman he was with, he started across the patio to Ann, his huge breadth of shoulder drawing her gaze and setting her core burning.

"I haven't seen you all night," Ann said in a voice much huskier than she'd intended. "I thought you'd be all over it, trying to get a piece now that I was back on the market." Ann saw the woman pulling the strap of her dress onto her shoulder. She adjusted her breasts before heading back inside.

Ann's confidence withered. "Ah." She looked back over the pool. "You didn't want to wait that long, I gather."

Charles' eyebrows pinched together as he glanced behind

him where the woman had been. "Oh no—she was just showing me her tits to try and get some."

"I'm amazed you could restrain yourself," Ann said with spice in her voice. She shook her head, trying to knock off the attitude. Her disappointment wasn't fair to Charles.

Before she could apologize for being an ass, Charles shrugged and leaned beside her. "She had a nice rack, but I've seen it before. Literally. A million times. I'm the last of Sasha's bodyguards to get tied down. They all want me."

"Should I step away—give your ego more room?"

"Nah. I'm bored with all the attention, now. At first it was cool. I mean, being a bodyguard was a shit job, right? It was embarrassing. But then she became a black mage, and the leader. Now I'm hot shit in this role. Even the humans want me—to get them knocked up, I mean. I can't find the thrill in it anymore, though. And I don't want to get attached to some human. They always expect to mate the father. Not interested."

"Wow. Hard life."

Charles sighed. "Yeah. I mean… look at me! I'm walking around the place like a freaking disco ball. I got most of it off, too, and still I shimmer. Jonas punches me every time he sees me."

Ann couldn't help laughing, her dour humor lifting despite herself.

"Oh sure, mock me. But do you get showered in glitter? Doubt it." Charles ran his fingers through his hair. "Anyway, I was giving you space. Sasha said you needed some *you* time. Needed to choose your guy, or whatever. I'd hate to distract you with the glitter arms."

Ann laughed harder. "Lemme see."

Grinning, Charles sauntered in front of her to give her a better view and put out one of his arms, which lit up like a

Christmas tree as the light played across the multi-colored glitter. "Sexy, am I right?"

"Is it all over?" Ann asked between large belly laughs.

"Yeah." He stripped off his shirt, exposing his broad shoulders and defined chest. Perfect pecs led down into a deliciously ripped six-pack—actually, almost an eight-pack. Tattoos swirled around his arms and dotted his torso.

Suddenly, she knew exactly why the girls had put glitter on him. That perfect body gleamed and sparkled. If he were in the throes of sex, it would also glisten. Her mouth turned dry as her fingers itched to touch that smooth skin, cut and defined in all the right ways. Tim had been muscular, too, but not like this. Charles was so tall and broad, so powerful, but sleek as well. He moved like a dancer. A lethal, efficient dancer.

"Light up your tattoos," Ann said in a breathy voice as her gaze roamed his torso.

Deep orange swirled around his arms, playful and light. The magic tickled her animal side, her magic responding to his in ways that were supposed to be completely foreign, but for some reason seemed as perfect as his body.

As his humor.

As his personality.

God she wanted this man. Had for years. She'd always said no to his advances because she knew she'd fall just that little bit more, and he didn't want to get attached. He'd just affirmed it a moment ago—not even a child would make him want to mate. He wanted his independence, and he wanted to bed whoever he chose, whenever he chose. Everyone in the Mansion knew that. It was only the humans who had a problem with it.

Ann sighed, feeling the fire as she looked over his delicious body. Then she came to a decision. Just this once, she wouldn't back away. Just this once, she'd give in to the thing he'd been trying to get from her since he first saw her.

She'd give in to him, just this once.

"Come closer, Charles," she said, suddenly a little nervous.

"With magic, or no?" He walked closer in that blasé way he could work so well, completely oblivious to the change in her bearing. To the heat she knew must be in her eyes.

"With."

He stopped in front of her, looking down at his torso before lifting his arms to get a better look. "You can't see the glitter when my tattoos light up. Maybe I should—"

She ran her palm up his chest, his words turning into a release of breath with the contact.

"Let's go back to when you said I looked pretty," Ann said, letting her fingers trail lightly down his abs.

The air between them warmed with their body heat. "Are you teasing me, Ann?" he asked quietly. "Because that would be a dick thing to do."

She put her other palm on his chest, feeling electricity jump between them from the increased contact. Her core sizzled and her feminine parts ached in need. She let her hands trail over his sides and to his back before applying the barest of pressure, seeing if he would respond as eagerly as she would.

He stepped toward her with her prompting, letting her lead. His hard length, contained in stylish pants, pushed up against her stomach. His hands fell to her hips.

"I've chosen," she whispered. "You. I hear you're great at making girls scream..."

"Ann," he said softly. His breath ruffled her hair. "You are so achingly beautiful, I couldn't keep my eyes off you when we were in the same room tonight. But you've never wanted this. I don't want to take advantage of you. You're hurting right now—I can wait until you're back to disgruntled and surly before I start trying to get in your pants again."

"Will you reject me tonight, Charles?" Ann tilted her face up to him.

His gaze roamed her face, resting on her lips. "Of course not. But we want different things. I don't want to hurt you."

"Tonight I don't care. Give me the dream, Charles, even if you have to pretend. Reality can ruin my day tomorrow."

Charles' hand came up. His thumb stroked her chin lightly as his face lowered slowly. His sweet breath dusted her eyelashes before his full lips glanced across hers.

A shock coursed through her body, pooling hot in her core. She sucked in a breath, leaning into him with trembling hands. His lips landed a little more firmly, but still light and teasing.

"I'll ask one more time—are you sure?" he mumbled against her lips.

"Yes." It was more a sigh than a word.

"Then let's go inside. Do you want anyone to know? I can go in after you, if you want. Keep it secret. Whatever you want."

"I don't care if they know. Hell, I'll be the envy of all the girls when I take you into a room with me."

Charles brushed her hair away from her face. "It's not like that with you, Ann. Don't cheapen this."

"Did you get that line from a romance novel?" she asked with a grin.

"Yeah. But it fits. Males feel this stuff, but we don't usually know what to say to prove it. Especially as females of my kind don't like to hear it. But I did some research for human girls when I first met Sasha."

"Cheater."

"Those romance books have some good shit in them. You seem like you need slow and sensual tonight, but if I get another shot, and you're back to surly, I've got dirty talk down for a hard... sexual experience. I mean, I know how to talk dirty, don't get me wrong. I'm a rock star. But thanks to those books, I can do it *sensually*."

Ann laughed, taking him by the hand and leading him toward the door. "A hard fuck. You can say it. It's not going to put me off right now."

"Next time."

"You won't get a next time." Ann led him through rooms with less people, hoping to avoid Sasha. She'd say this was a bad idea, that Ann would definitely get hurt if she gave Charles any more of her heart. But Ann didn't want to be safe tonight. She just wanted to have what she wanted. Multiple times. She'd deal with the repercussions tomorrow.

"Oh, I'll get a next time. You're giving me pity sex tonight —which I thank you for, by the way—but when you're back to your normal self, I've got some tricks. I'm going to rock your world."

Ann smiled as they climbed the stairs, Charles receiving the attention of every female. He wasn't lying—he was heavily sought after, and it showed.

But tonight *she* was getting him.

CHAPTER THREE

Ann had butterflies as Charles closed the door behind them. He looked around the room at the bed, the dresser, and various other guest room items. Ann stayed there a couple of times a week, so it was a little more lived-in than most of the other guest rooms in the house.

He went to the nightstand and pulled open the drawer.

"I'm on the pill—I don't have any condoms here," she said, drawing the shades over the brightening day.

"I was looking for candles." He glanced up, his striking face claiming her focus. And then his body glittered with remnants of whatever he had done last night.

"I'll just leave the blinds open a crack. Since, you know, the sun is like one big, massive candle..." She made a show of lifting the shades a fraction so a spear of light could pierce the murky darkness.

"Sunlight isn't romantic. Flickering candle-light is the way to go." He tsked, walking toward her slowly. Her hackles rose, sensing the predatory nature of his species. The same qualities that matched her animal side. "As a human female, I would expect you to know that basic trivia."

"I've been seduced, Charles. You don't have to try so hard."

He grinned as he reached her, lightly running his fingertips down her cheek. His breath, slow and deep, mingled with hers, which was shallow and erratic. She couldn't seem to get enough air.

"Females are like fine wines—you have to be patient," he said in a slow, deep voice. He bent to her neck, kissing her ever so softly. A tease. "You have to start slow, letting it open up. Letting the air mix with it, relax it, and let the flavor out."

His lips trailed down her neck, tickling. His hot breath ran the length of her collarbone. "When it's ready, and not before, you have to set the tone to fully enjoy it. You have to get the mood just right—play on the expectation." His lips dotted her chest, barely touching her skin.

She leaned her head back as her body tingled. Her core sizzled with flame. All she could think about was his touch, barely there. Teasing her.

"If you take your time with the wine, and let it open up just right, you'll be rewarded with a punch of flavor to rival any other." His fingers played over her shoulders, touching down for a moment. The fabric of her dress pulled just a bit before the silk of her straps drifted over her shoulders and down her arms. Red silk whispered as it slid over her curves and pooled at her feet.

Hot breath moved over her bare breasts, making her break out in goosebumps. A scorching tongue just barely touched her budded nipple.

Ann's eyes fluttered as a moan escaped her lips.

"Females love to be tortured," Charles whispered, the moist heat of his tongue flicking her nipple again.

"Ooh, Charles," she breathed, shivers wracking her body.

"Do you want to be tied up?" he asked. "I can focus solely on you tonight if you need me to."

That expert, playful tongue flicked the other nipple. A jolt of pleasure vibrated her body.

She'd been tied up before, and it had been fairly useless. The idea was always better than the outcome. Something told her, though, that Charles would be an exception. He would play her like a fiddle for hours, driving her to the brink before backing off, forcing her to writhe and plead and beg for mercy, all the while hoping he didn't give it.

But tonight, she wanted to touch him. To hold him while he moved inside her.

"Okay," he said quietly, somehow getting his answer without her having to give it.

A soft touch slid down her sides and hovered over her panties. His hot tongue circled her nipple, giving her another thrill of shivers as his hands flattened over her hips. She felt his thumbs apply pressure as his tongue flicked her again. Another moan escaped her lips.

Without warning, his mouth enveloped her nipple as her panties were pulled down her thighs. She arched with an "Oh!", clutching onto his meaty shoulders. The suction intensified as the chill of the room assaulted her hot, wet sex.

His hand kneaded the other breast. Fingers slid between her lower lips, parting her folds. "Hmm, you're wet," he breathed, moving his mouth up her chest and kissing her neck.

Ann moaned, running her hands over his warm, muscled shoulders before snaking around his neck. One of his hands cupped her cheek as the other applied pressure between her thighs. His lips were on hers again, lacking the smooth finesse he'd shown a moment before. This time, as his tongue ran along her bottom lip, she felt his urgency. Felt his need for her.

It was so much hotter than the slow torture.

She opened her mouth, moaning when he filled it in a

rush. A digit dipped into her body, curved to hit her inner walls just right. She ran a hand up his neck before running her fingers into his hair, gripping a handful and giving a small yank. His kiss deepened as a masculine groan sounded deep in his throat.

Another finger joined the first inside her while his thumb traced lazy circles at the top of her slit, sending shooting sparks of pleasure through her body. His other hand pinched a nipple before rubbing it, ecstasy blistering through her.

"Oh," she moaned into his mouth.

In a quick movement, he bent and scooped her up into his arms, cradling her against his chest, his lips not leaving hers. He walked to the bed where she felt his muscles bunch before she experienced one moment of weightlessness. Her body flew through the air as she squealed in surprise. She landed on the mattress, arms out, legs splayed, a desirous grin taking over her face.

"You are so fucking sexy, Ann. A huge prude, but so fucking sexy."

She giggled as he crawled onto the bed after her, eyes blazing, tattoos swirling with color. His magic flirted with hers as his hands gripped her upper thighs and pushed, spreading her legs further apart, demanding access. His face dipped in before his mouth ran up her slit.

"Oh fuck," she gasped, jolting backwards and arching.

He ran his tongue around her clit in lazy, delicious circles. Fingers dipped into her body, not exactly in sync, but somehow so much better because of it. His other hand was on her breast, kneading to yet another rhythm, which perfectly complimented what he was doing with the other parts of her body.

Her breath caught in her throat. Her heart hammered. Her eyes fluttered. Her toes curled as she clawed at the sheets, arching so high she would make a yoga master proud.

All the while her body wound up so fucking tight she wanted to yell at him to stop. She couldn't take it. The thick, heady pleasure pounded her, wave after excruciating wave. Pleasure so sharp it cut through her body. It was too much. It felt too good. She couldn't—

"Oh FUCK!" she screamed as her entire body blasted apart. Light danced behind her eyes before everything went black; the only thing she could focus on were the waves of indescribable pleasure rocketing through her and setting her on fire.

Panting heavily, sweat covering her body, tremors racking her, she lay still for a moment. Feeling what it was like to be electrocuted from the inside out by the best damn orgasm she'd ever had, in her entire life.

A soft kiss pressed against her navel.

Fingers trailed lightly from the side of her knee up the inside of her thighs.

She didn't know if she could carry on.

As if reading her mind, she heard a dark chuckle, and then a flick of a tongue against her clit.

"No!" Ann jolted, her hands flying to Charles' shoulders, ready to restrain him. She was still too sensitive for any more of those shenanigans.

The next kiss fell on her inner thigh, soft and sweet. Letting her catch her breath.

She didn't think that would ever happen.

Another tremor slid through her body, making her shiver with an aftershock of that incredible orgasm.

"It's not your position they are after, Charles. It's your mouth."

"Who, the females?"

"No. The bedbugs," she said sarcastically.

Suction found her clit again, hard and intense. She yelped as her body jolted, the sensations unbearable with sensitivity.

She pushed at his shoulders, moaning again, eyes squeezed shut, not sure if she wanted him to stop or suck harder.

It hurt so fucking good.

Her fingers turned into claws, digging into his flesh as spicy tingles of pleasure needled up her skin. His fingers plunged inside of her, pushing out a groan. Blissful pain accosted her, just barely on the side of pleasure.

"No, Charles," she begged in a frantic moan, legs at odds with her statement as she hooked her heels behind his powerful arms and held him in place. "Oh Charles, I can't."

Her hips gyrated up into his mouth as his fingers slammed into her, hard and forceful, pushing past the wall of over-sensitivity. "Oh God. Oh God. Oh no. No, no. Ohhh." Ann gripped a handful of his hair and rocked her hips into him, coming off the bed. She scratched his shoulder with the other hand, needing to harm him somehow as the unbearable sensations pounded her. Her body lit on fire for the second time, but this time it blistered. Her breathing caught up in time with the wild, frantic swinging of her hips. Her body wound up, so tight. So hard.

"Oh Charles, oh God, oh—"

Everything stopped. His face ripped away. His fingers disappeared.

"What the *fuck?*" she breathed in agony, right on the edge. Right on the very edge of an extremely high cliff of unbearable pleasure.

She struggled up to her elbows to look down between her legs, but he'd risen up. Smoky grey eyes burning with fire rooted to hers. He yanked open his fly and pushed down his trousers. His huge erection bobbed free, his species packing heavy and he no exception.

Her chest heaved as her gaze raked his glistening, sparkling body, the glitter looking like little explosions with each movement. She couldn't help a small laugh as he tossed his pants to the floor.

"You shouldn't laugh when a guy reveals his junk, Ann." Charles scowled when she laughed harder. "You'll pay for that."

"Oh yeah, how is that?" she taunted, still on fire. Wanting to pin him to the mattress and bite him as she slammed her body down on top of his.

Eyes sparkling with mischief, he slowly bent between her legs, his gaze still connected with hers, his tongue came out and wiggled her clit. Sparks of shooting pleasure pierced her body, reminding her of that cliff, of her need for just a little more friction to jump off.

He wiggled just a bit more, sending her closer. And then closer still. All she needed was a suck. A hard suck, and she'd be over.

He softly blew on her. "Beg me to let you come."

"Fuck you, Charles!" She gritted her teeth against the agony.

He blew softly again, his breath cool against her fevered sex. The contrast made her insides squeeze with need. Aching torture had her hips pushing up to him, needing his mouth.

"Beg me, Ann. Beg me to let you come. I want a pretty please with it, too."

She sat up in a rush, grabbing his shoulders and attempting to throw him to the mattress. He didn't even budge. Impossible strength held him, not even needing to wrestle back. He just hung out with a smug smile, his eyes sparkling like the glitter on his body.

He tsked. "Nope. You need to beg. That, or say you're sorry for laughing at my cock."

"I wasn't laughing at your cock," she ground out through clenched teeth, struggling to rip him to the side again. She was way stronger than humans—shifters naturally were and she'd worked on strength training. She should at least be able to knock him off-balance. "I was laughing at your glitter."

"Hmm. Well, joke's on you. I'm having fun. Beg me."

She fell back to the bed and threw on a pout. "I thought you were going to make this all about me? I'm having a tough time…"

His smile dwindled. He watched her for a minute, his gaze dipping to her downturned lips before he sighed softly. "You win."

His hands slid firmly along the inside of her thighs to the crease. He bent and slowly ran his lips up the line of her sex, tickling her slit open before playfully flicking her clit. But it was too soft, too teasing. If anything, it was ten times worse than doing nothing at all.

"Harder Charles," she instructed, shivers spreading across her body once again, heat rushing in after.

He gave her feather-light touches, increasing the uncomfortable need to orgasm. "Charles—!"

"Pretty please…" he whispered.

She couldn't help an agonized grin. He'd called her bluff. "I hate that you know me so well!"

"With sugar on top…" The next feather-touch made her groan in frustration.

"Fine. Please. Pretty please. With a mountain of sugar. *Please* let me come, Charles."

"Good girl." He sucked her in, *hard*. His fingers entered her body, curving just right, before starting a rhythm. Almost immediately, and without warning, an orgasm ripped through her, jolting her back onto the bed and making her whole body go taut. She couldn't even sigh. Or yell. She vibrated, electrocuted again, clutching onto his shoulders as her eyes rolled back into her head.

She managed a ragged breath and a "thank you."

He kissed up her body, nipping her occasionally, causing

her to groan. He didn't linger anywhere, not even on her nipples. Instead, he reached her lips and kissed her deeply, resting his large body on top of hers. His manhood ran up her slit, pressing against her.

She moaned as she ran her palms over his shoulders and entwined her fingers around his neck. His tongue entered her mouth as his hands ran the length of her body. He grabbed her behind her right knee and hoisted her leg higher on his hip. Lips staying connected, with sensual body movements, he rose up a fraction until his tip slid down the center of her sex. When it met her opening, he pushed forward slowly.

Her eyes fluttered as his girth slowly entered her body. "Oh," she sighed into his mouth.

"I've wanted this for a long time, Ann," he said softly.

"So have I," she admitted, kissing him. She slid her knees further up to rest high on his hips.

He continued to push into her, the feeling of his body inside hers making her exhale noisily. The glorious stretch turned into a dull ache, her body not used to his size. Without needing to be told, he paused before backing back out, letting her relax for a moment.

The man was a sex magician. He knew what she needed, how hard she needed it, and when, without her ever having to open her mouth. Or, more correctly, without her having to break from moaning like a ghost in an attic.

After a moment of just kissing, his hips rocked forward again, making it halfway this time before her body screeched for him to stop. He backed off again, the kiss turning languid, before working in farther, and a little more, never pushing too much. Never rushing. He had more control than anyone she'd ever heard of.

Before the final plunge, he grabbed her hands and gently moved them up, above her head. His fingers threaded into hers. His hips rocked forward, his girth sliding into her, filling her up.

"Mmm." She squeezed his middle with her thighs, rocking her hips up just that little more to take him completely. To surround his length with her body.

"Gods, you feel good. So tight," Charles breathed, resting his forehead lightly onto hers. "You have to give me a moment. I'm not... completely in control right now."

"That's okay," she whispered, clenching and releasing him with her body.

"I've been so turned on for so long that I'll only have one shot before I need to recoup. I have to make it count. Which you are making impossible with the... *oh*, with the muscle gymnastics. Ann. Stop. You're killing me. Give me a..."

Charles flexed, bearing down on her, pushing her body deeper into the mattress. His breathing became labored, struggling for control.

"Just let go," Ann murmured, rocking against him as much as she could, contracting her inner muscles. Even without a lot of movement, he was so big, filling her up to capacity that her body was already winding tighter.

"This is... supposed to be slow... and steady..." he panted, squeezing her hands.

"I want you, Charles," Ann purred, eyes closed, milking his girth. "Please, Charles," she whispered breathily into his ear.

"Ah gawds you're so damn sexy—"

The dam burst. He pulled back before *thrusting* into her, slamming against her body. She gasped.

He withdrew again before thrusting, ripping a moan from her throat. He pulled out, and this time she rocked up as he bore down, his hard slide rubbing just right.

"Oh God," she moaned, approaching the edge again. Her hips swung up savagely as he crashed down, their rhythm frantic and wild, straining toward each other. The bed squeaked from his rhythmic thrusts. Their hands gripped each other in a desperate hold.

"Oh Ann—Gods Ann. Are you close? At all?"

At that place where reality and time didn't exist, ruled by sensation, Ann could only nod helplessly as her body braced on the edge of the largest cliff yet. She reveled in his body sliding against hers, slippery and wet from their exertions. His lips trailing down her neck, soft despite his hard thrusts and she felt his movement inside her, filling her in a way no one else ever had. He squeezed out sensations she hadn't even imagined a person could feel.

Something pinched at her neck, a sharp pain that made her suck in her breath. A deep pull reached down through the very core of her, tied directly to her sex. Unbelievable bliss spread throughout her body as the pull happened again, yanking a whimper of unparalleled delight from her lips. Her mouth dropped open as her mind detached from her body, floating somewhere on a sea of ecstasy that could not have been real. It was so raw and pure.

Her mouth rounded into an "O" as one more pull yanked at her, stealing her breath. For one stomach churning moment, she teetered on the edge of stinging anguish, her body so tightly wound it hurt.

"Oh!" The wave broke, sucking her under. An orgasm so intense she utterly blacked out. She might've screamed, or begged, or cried—she had no idea. All she felt was Charles' body quaking, his hands holding hers, and him inside of her. All she heard was him calling her name as he climaxed. All she knew was him.

CHAPTER FOUR

All the strength left Charles as he collapsed on top of Ann. He was twice her size and probably three times her weight with the muscle ratio, and yet, he couldn't move to get off of her. His limbs were jello.

He'd been with females for entire days at a time who had made him climax three and four times, each more extreme than the last, building on each other. None of them, not one, had ever been this extreme. They'd never taken him this high, or made him lose control this readily.

Charles wasn't sure he liked it. Yes, it felt fucking amazing, but a male shouldn't lose control like that. He'd taken her blood without asking, for cripes-sakes. That would probably come back to bite him.

He licked his lips languidly, tasting the sweet blood on his lips. Another zing from that magical elixir fired within him.

He'd never heard of anyone taking blood from a shifter. He had no idea it would be so different. So… weird.

It was freaking exhilarating, if he was being honest. It fired through his body, giving him impressions of dense wood, wildness, and raw senses. It played off his predatory nature.

He could get addicted to her blood.

Reluctantly he rolled to the side so he was mostly off of her body. She didn't so much as twitch. If he hadn't been able to see the amazing display of her breasts rising and falling, he'd think she was dead.

Fuck, that was a good lay.

He should really get up and go to the guest room reserved for him. His job here was done.

Except, she smelled really good, and her presence was pleasing. They'd been on enough excursions and missions with Sasha that they knew each other really well. It made things between them... easy. Comfortable. But, he was so tired.

That was the nice thing about doing a friend—he didn't have to worry about her getting the wrong idea. They could cuddle without it becoming a big deal.

Charles snuggled up beside her, not bothering to pull the blankets over them. He was too tired.

And they'd definitely be doing this again. With sex this good, this was the start of a friends-with-benefits arrangement. She'd ended his streak of boredom and there was no way he was going to let that go even if she wanted to be prudish. Out of the question.

Charles sighed in contentment as he hugged her close and fell deeply asleep.

∼

The next evening Charles awoke to a warm body and the smell of bacon. He was still wrapped around Ann, spooning her from behind, the blankets still beneath them. He hadn't woken up once during the day.

Huh.

That was unusual when he shared a sleeping space with someone.

As morning wood stiffened his member, he ran his lips down Ann's neck, breathing in her sweet elixir of the wilds and female. *Great gods she smells good.*

He ran his hand up the front of her, cupping a firm breast and smiling when her nipple constricted, poking his palm. He should really get up and make sure everything was ready for them to leave in a few hours, but...

He sucked in the skin over the beating pulse in her neck as he reached between her thighs. As his middle finger parted her folds, she gave a soft moan, spreading her legs. He dipped his finger into her, loving the immediate wetness from his touch. Without delay, he grabbed his dick by the base and aimed his tip at her opening, rubbing to spread her slickness.

"Oh..." she sighed, pushing her butt into his groin before lifting a leg and reaching it back to hook behind him.

In other words, get to it.

He slid into her tightness, his breath leaving his lungs in a sudden exhalation. Just like the night before, the urgency came on him. He couldn't keep a slow pace without losing his mind. Everything in him said to pump as hard and fast as he could, filling her completely and making her his.

A blast of fear burst through him with that feeling, but was quickly overshadowed with pleasure. He moved his fingers over her nub in fast circles as he thrust. He groaned as he pulled out and thrust again, harder this time. He needed her. Had to have her.

Thought fled. Control followed.

He rolled onto her and pulled back on her hips, propping her up doggy-style so he could take her harder. So he could completely dominate her.

Hands clutching her smooth hips, noticing her fingers

curl into the sheets as she held on, he pumped into her, as deep as he could go. Harder now, crashing down as he pulled her hips back, taking her.

"Oh Charles, please," she begged. She dug her head into the pillow while clutching harder at the sheets, submitting to his desires.

A thrill went through him, like closing in on a kill. Or claiming a female.

He thrust his hips forward, slapping off her. Pounding into her. Urgency rose higher as an unbelievable sensation overcame him, blocking out that earlier frisson of fear.

He pulled her up by her hair, loving the sweet moan that escaped her lips. He licked down her neck until he found her pulse, and then cut a small opening with his teeth. As hot blood tumbled over his tongue, he sucked in deep, the sensation of dominance growing. Overcoming him. Stealing his breath.

"Oh, holy—" Ann cut off, her fingers clutching his thighs now.

The thrill of wildness washed through his senses once again, just like the night before. Stalking prey, battling, and the glory of victory had his eyes fluttering. The base of his cock tingled and his gut tightened.

He barely stopped himself from taking a second pull from her vein. If he kept at it, he'd bleed her dry.

He wrapped his arms around her chest, squeezing her into him as he thrust wildly, needing more. Needing everything.

Fear flooded through him once again. He'd sworn he wouldn't reduce his options by committing to one female. That wasn't what his culture did. They remained open and available.

Fighting his own desires, desperate not to give in, he clung onto her, pressing his face into her sweet smelling neck. He pumped harder, his breath ragged, his instincts screaming at him to give her blood and initiate a link.

"How close?" he begged Ann. "I need to finish."

Ann reached down and touched herself, working up more sensation.

"Oh gods," Charles groaned, the act of a prudish girl touching herself sending him over the edge.

Another catastrophic orgasm crashed over him, dragging him under. Her interior muscles started firing a moment later, squeezing and pulling and milking him in an impossibly tight grip. She moaned, shuddering in his arms. He shook with her as he pumped her full of his essence.

Another longing accosted him. One of procreation. Of creating a piece of himself for the next generation. He desperately wanted to get her pregnant.

"What the hell is happening to me?" Charles muttered, backing away.

She collapsed onto the bed, her face deep into the pillow. "Don't know. Don't care. I'm exhausted."

Charles knelt on the bed for a moment, staring down at her perfect body. He shook his head, hating the soft fuzzies warming his insides.

These feelings were just because of their friendship. Had to be. They had a solid foundation of trust, and lots of laughs. Now he was getting confused and losing his mind. He wasn't like the Boss or Jonas, giving in to the humans' culture of being tied down to one female. No way. He was a rogue warrior. Mr Magical Dick, that was him. Everyone in the Mansion knew it.

Nodding to himself, Charles slid off the bed and lifted her gently. Her arms snaked around his neck and her face rested on his shoulder. He felt her warm breath against his neck.

"Stop it. Quit breathing on me." He held her tightly with one hand so he could rip back the covers.

"You're ruining my chi. Shut it," she mumbled.

He settled her into the soft covers and pulled the blankets up over her. "You have a couple hours, then we have to go. I hope you're packed."

"I am. I don't wait until the last minute to do things, unlike you. And don't bring that horrid blanket you're making. It doesn't even have a defined shape."

"Shows what you know. It's going to be a wrap."

"No. It's going to be something used to clean up baby puke."

"That's useful, too."

Ann snorted and snuggled deeper into the pillows. The pull to get in beside her had Charles stepping forward. The confusion of wanting to hang out in bed with a female when there was work to be done had him scowling and moving back again.

Things were getting a bit lopsided.

He snatched up his clothes and stalked out of the bedroom. No way was a chick going to make him think that great sex meant marital bondage. That only happened to the chicks.

Except maybe Jonas. And the Boss. And possibly Paulie.

Scowling harder, Charles made his way down to the kitchen. Jonas stood beside the center island, watching Jessenta, who was in charge of organizing household duties for Sasha and the Boss, make breakfast for anyone that wanted it. Sasha sat at the small, round table in the corner, eating a piece of toast.

"We're going to be taking off in two or three hours," Charles said as he grabbed some OJ out of the fridge.

"Oh. I didn't know you were here. Where'd you sleep?" Sasha asked. "And why are you carrying your clothes instead of wearing them?"

"Walk of shame." Jonas grinned as he took a sip of his

coffee. "Had to get out of bed before the female woke up. Or females, plural."

Charles rolled his shoulders and sucked in a surge of magic, his fighting instincts going active. He had no idea why.

The wildness of Ann's blood zinged through him again, making the draw of magic a little sweeter, and a little more exotic.

"Whoa." Sasha leaned forward, eyes glued to Charles' arms. "Who were you with last night?"

"More importantly, whose blood did you take?" Jonas asked.

Charles looked down at his glowing tattoos as the Boss walked in. Instead of orange, his default color, or light gold, which was what he pulled when Sasha increased his magic flow, he was burnished gold, the magic power right before stepping up into white. It was the Boss' power level, and pretty damn potent.

"Ann," Charles said softly, cutting off the magic.

"Wait." Sasha dropped her toast onto the plate in front of her. "You slept with *Ann* last night?"

"I didn't know shifters could boost power like that," the Boss said, standing in the entryway to the kitchen. "How much did you take?"

"No, the real question is: how could you, Charles?" Sasha's voice had raised an octave. The hair on Charles' neck stood on end before more power seeped into him, the gold turning extremely dark. Sasha's magic was on the move. That was not a good thing.

"Calm down, babe," the Boss said in an easy tone often needed when Sasha's hormones became active. And crazy. "Charles wouldn't take advantage of her." The Boss' dominating, and terrifying, gaze smacked into Charles, making it clear that Charles had better not have taken advantage.

Charles threw up his hands in surrender. "She chose me. I

tried to talk her out of it, but she asked if I would reject her. I figured saying no would be worse than yes."

"No, it wouldn't have been," Sasha argued. "She was sad, half-drunk, and horny. *Obviously* she was into it. But you know she likes you, Charles. And you also know she wants monogamy. If you are half as good as people say you are, she probably likes you even more now. It's only going to hurt more when she realizes you are a slut and she'll never get you."

"I doubt she'd want you telling him all this," Jonas rumbled.

"I am absolutely as good as people say I am!" Jonas snorted as Charles drank OJ straight out of the container, just to piss Sasha off. "But you're overreacting. If she liked me, she would've given in before now. She just let down her guard last night, and this morning she was back to her usual snarly self. And guess what? I'm going to try and lay her again. So suck it."

Charles expected the Boss to reprimand him. When he didn't, tingles of fearful anticipation worked up his spine.

It meant something worse was coming.

His body slammed back against the refrigerator. Bands of black scorched into his skin, locking him in place. Electricity shocked him, forcing out rapid breaths of pain.

Charles drew in more magic, as much as he could, smelling whiffs of forest and feeling the thrill of the hunt. The black bands smoked a little, weakening. His magic was unfurling the spells.

The electric shock turned up in intensity, the spells shifting and solidifying, making him grunt. She wanted an apology.

She was not going to get it. He had enough weird shit going on with Ann that he didn't need a third party trying to play police.

"His magic is reacting differently," Jonas said. Apparently he didn't much care that Charles was frying against the refrigerator. "Do shifters have varying degrees of power, like we do?"

"Yes," the Boss answered, doing nothing to stop his insane mate. Charles would be damned if he'd beg. Not this time. Hopefully. "You can see it in their hierarchy. Tim has the strongest magic. Which makes sense since he's the alpha. Ann must be pretty high up there, though. She's near the top of their hierarchy, no matter what the situation is."

"Are you going to apologize to her?" Sasha asked in a deathly quiet voice.

"This is none of your business, Sasha," Charles ground out through clenched teeth.

"I didn't know their magic could mesh with ours, though," Jonas reflected. "Does she have a higher level than Charles, or is it just the effect of the two combining?"

"What's going on?" Ann asked in a sleepy voice as she sauntered into the kitchen. She was wearing a small tank top and no bra, capturing Charles' attention immediately.

Her breasts were so perky and perfect. And the soft moans she made when he sucked on them...

Jonas snorted and took a sip of his coffee as Sasha's magic fell away. Charles staggered forward before he could catch himself, the seared skin from her magic now throbbing. As was his hard cock.

"Punishment fits the crime," Jonas said in a rasp, snagging a piece of bacon off the plate Jessenta laid on the counter.

"I can think of better punishments than that," Sasha grumbled. "But I'd ruin the kitchen."

"Wasn't talking about that punishment. Good morning, mongrel. Sleep well?" Jonas snagged another piece of bacon and headed toward the doorway, saying to Charles, "Hurry up, child. I'm your ride to the Mansion. You finally got a car.

Congratulations. Soon you'll need it to tote around your kids."

A thrill of both excitement and fear fired through Charles. His eyebrows lowered in response, noticing the dark eyes of the Boss on him. He met that gaze, not caring if it was seen as a challenge. He didn't want kids yet, at least not ones he had to help to raise. If some female wanted a little sperm as a donation, fine, but no leash would be applied to his nuts because of it.

"Nice glitter, Ann," Sasha said with assessing eyes.

Ann glanced at her chest and arms before shrugging. "I finally shagged the naked idiot leaking orange juice all over the floor. His party decor rubbed off."

"What are you taking with you tonight?" the Boss asked, sitting next to Sasha.

Ann glanced at Charles before sticking out her hand for the orange juice. She did a double-take, her gaze snapping back to his like a rubber band. "You okay, killer?"

Charles handed over the orange juice. "Yep." He brushed past her and snagged a piece of bacon. "Boss, I'll talk to you at the Mansion."

As he was leaving the kitchen, he heard Sasha ask, "Are you okay?"

She wasn't talking to him, she was talking to Ann.

Despite himself, Charles slowed as he rounded the corner.

"Great. He is a fan-tast-ic lay. *Fantastic.* Best I've had, and I don't even care if it boosts his ego. That's how good."

"But... you're not... upset that he doesn't want anything else?" Sasha persisted.

A chair scraped against the tile. "I knew that going in. It's fine. I scratched an itch, I know what's behind door number three, and I'm good."

"Huh. Well. Okay, then. Are you going to do it again?"

Charles started as the Boss' big shoulders appeared around the corner. Charles was walking as soon as he could get his legs moving, but the tweak in the Boss' lips said he knew Charles was eavesdropping.

When a bad situation gets worse...

"I thought you were going to find out what she's taking tonight?" Charles asked as the Boss caught up with him.

"I will when she's done talking to Sasha. You got everything ready?"

They walked through the empty living room. "Yeah—where're the kids?"

"They're at the park with Emmy and Selene. What did Jameson scrounge up technology-wise?"

They left the house. Jonas stood next to his Hummer, staring out at nothing. The male was a cranky ol' sod, but he could do patience like nobody's business. He just... shut off, somehow.

"I have a device to deaden communication. It'll cut out cell phones, walkie-talkies, any surveillance traveling through the air-waves..."

"Anything else?"

Jonas looked over as they approached the car.

"I also have a coded cell phone that *may* work around a device of theirs that cuts out communication," Charles continued. "Jameson doesn't have faith that the nerds got that one right."

The Boss leaned against the Hummer. "We hacked into the nearest satellite and were able to get an image before we were kicked out again. It's a large facility sprawling within the mountains. Looks high-tech. We didn't see any elaborate defense. Just a fence and a few dogs."

"They have to have something to catch shifters, though," Jonas spoke up. "Tim's people are good. They wouldn't have fallen into a trap. If all of them were taken, it means this facility has something shifters can't get away from. Something they wouldn't see when sneaking close."

"The question is, is that something going to affect non-shifters?" The Boss looked at Charles. "I'm giving you a week. After that, we're coming in after you. I want you calling every few hours if you can. Feed us information as you get it. You have the maps?"

"Yes. The cottage is cleaned out of humans?" Charles opened his door as Jonas walked around the other side of the car. Time to go.

"It was already empty. The man who owns it is elderly. He used to use it as a summer cabin years ago. He has no family to pass the cabin on to, so we've established ourselves as his next of kin. His estate will be a nice source of income in a few years."

"Probably shouldn't tell Sasha all that." Charles climbed into the plush, leather seat.

"She's okay as long as the person in question doesn't have kids." The Boss stepped away. "We have to keep funding our operation somehow..."

Jonas turned the ignition and the vehicle roared to life. Charles gave a salute and closed the door. As the Hummer pulled away, Jonas said, "So... it was good, but now it's fucking with your mind?"

Charles knew exactly what he was talking about. *Who* he was talking about. And he didn't want to discuss it. "Focused on the job."

Jonas snorted. "Time to put on your big boy pants. Your balls are dropping, finally. Couldn't pick better, either. She's a solid female who would rip someone's throat out to keep her pack safe. That's good people, even if she has a terrible sense of humor."

"That makes two of you."

Jonas snorted again, and thankfully let it lie. There were other things to be worried about. Like a lab that was snatching shifters.

The question was, did they only catch shifters, or were they welcoming to all...

CHAPTER FIVE

Charles pulled up at the shifter compound, a bunch of bungalows in the woods, and rolled down his window. They had another place located nearer the city but, from what Charles could gather, this acted as more of a headquarters.

A few people stood near the main facility where the long gravel driveway ended. Ann had a big duffle bag lying on the ground as she faced Tim. Charles couldn't hear what she said, but he saw her shrug, and get a warm hug.

Charles glanced off to the side as a strange, violent reaction coursed through him. It must've been Ann's blood.

From the corner of his eye, he saw her hug someone else, then another, saying goodbye to her pack-mates. A few minutes later, the passenger door opened.

"Hey." Ann climbed in as the trunk opened. Tim put her duffle in the back.

"Hi."

"New wheels?"

Tim appeared on Charles' side with a stern face and hard eyes. Charles rolled down the window and lifted his eyebrows. He'd never been stand-offish with the bear alpha before, but...

It had to be Ann's blood. It was really distracting.

"Stay safe," Tim said. "If anything looks wrong, get out of there. We want to get a feeling of what we're up against, not lose two more."

"If they take us, there'll be a pissed-off mage in the height of crazy pregnancy hormones showing up at their door. I wouldn't wish that on anybody."

Tim smirked and nodded, stepping away. "Not to mention an angry Kodiak. Good luck."

Charles turned the car around, and headed out, pulling out the map and resting it on Ann's knees. "Got everything?"

"Yeah. You?"

"Yup."

"You leave that horrible excuse for a wrap behind?"

"I did." Charles pulled out onto the main road. "Instead, I brought the makings of a dog blanket. I figured it would work for an overgrown kitty-cat, as well."

"Why didn't you just say cat blanket?" Ann pulled a flashlight out of her pocket and clicked it on. She looked at the map.

"Cats have blankets?"

He barely saw her shrug. "Anyway, when do you need me to start navigating?"

Charles vaguely pointed to the dashboard where the GPS was guiding them. "When that thing loses service."

Ann glanced at the dash before looking around the large SUV. "Big car. If I wasn't so sore, I'd ask if you were compensating for something."

Tingles filtered through Charles' stomach and pooled at the base of his dick, making him half-hard. "How sore, exactly?"

"Don't even bother. Been there, done that. Time to move on."

"That's what they all say. Lies."

"I doubt it. Your kind don't really move on, do they? They just hang around with their legs spread, hoping for a poke." Ann laughed at her own joke before running her fingers along the dash. "So how come you had to wait so long before getting your own wheels?"

Charles turned onto the highway. "We don't need cars littering the Mansion. There are vehicles for common use, and there are certain people nominated to drive if we all need to get somewhere. As the Watch Captain on my own detail, looks like the Boss decided I needed to be included as one of the drivers."

"Who picked this ride?"

"I just said I wanted something Sasha wouldn't want to drive."

"Ah." Ann laughed as she took her phone from a small satchel on the floor. "Yeah, if you got something fast, she'd push you over and take control."

"Exactly. The Boss won't even get her a new car—hers is fast for an old ride, but if she got her hands on something faster..."

"Like Stefan's..."

"The Boss has a special switch on that. She can't drive it unless she knows the code, and the Boss won't tell her. Or anyone else."

Ann shook her head with a big smile. "It's for the best, but that would piss me off."

"Pisses her off too, but there are some things you just don't push where the Boss is concerned. That applies even to her."

"Well, I'm going to read now. Quit your yapping."

"Oh. Great. Surly Ann is back."

"Yup. Now you can talk dirty all you want."

"Fancy a fuck?"

Ann laughed and squinted down at her phone. Clearly she hadn't thought he was serious.

They arrived at the cabin as the sun was peeking out over the horizon. Judging by the map, they were a good distance down the mountain from the facility. A tiny road, partly overgrown, led to the front of a small square building made of logs. It looked like the picture on the front of Log Cabin syrup. An old, decrepit porch swing squeaked as it swayed gently in the breeze.

"Home sweet home," Ann said in a dry voice as she climbed out of the SUV.

Charles followed her, meeting her in front of the hood and putting an arm to stop her forward progress. "Let me go in and check it out, just in case."

"I don't smell any people or strange scents."

"I think if danger was obvious, half your pack wouldn't be missing." He took out his sword and approached the door slowly, letting his magic unfurl and coat the ground, looking for magical traps of any kind. After three years of developing his skill, he could manage twenty feet, a rough semblance of the spell Sasha could use for miles. Still, it worked great for that twenty feet.

He tried the door handle, finding it unlocked. He didn't bother reaching for the keys someone had obtained from the human who owned this place. Pushing the door open, a sparse, mostly empty space greeted him, smelling dank and musty.

Charles let his magic tumble across the floor ahead of him. He didn't see anybody or any other magic. After a quick check in the bathroom, he walked back out to Ann, who was facing East with her eyes closed, standing perfectly still.

"If that's yoga, you're doing it wrong." Charles moved around the SUV to get the luggage.

"The breeze is rolling off the mountain. Something smells... really delicious. It's extremely faint, though."

"Smells like me, then?"

"Despite its popularity, I don't find the aroma of ball sweat particularly enjoyable..."

Charles hefted their bags and moved toward the cabin. Ann crossed to the back of the SUV.

"Leave it—I can get it." Charles sighed when she grabbed the last bag and closed the trunk behind her.

"This must have the tech in it. Of *course* you leave the heavy one for me."

"I did just say to leave it."

"Listening to you is a bad habit I don't want to develop. I've lasted this long, I wouldn't want to ruin my track record on one mission."

Charles dropped the luggage next to the bed and gave another glance around. "That one has some tech, and all the groceries."

Ann opened the bag and went through the items as Charles looked down at the round table between the fireplace and kitchen. Everything in here was close together. The place was no more than ten feet by fifteen. There was not a lot of space.

The table was filthy.

Charles spotted a towel hanging on an empty dish rack but even that was covered in heavy dust. He turned to the sink. The faucet sputtered a couple times as he turned it on before coughing to life. The water at least looked clear and clean.

"Looks like it works. The man said as much, but Jameson thought he was mostly senile." Charles put the dirty rag under the stream of water, grimacing as brown liquid coated the bottom of the kitchen sink.

He shut off the water before looking in the cabinets under the sink. Finding a little pail, which was being used as a garbage can, he threw the disgusting towel in and closed the cabinet. Next he stripped off his shirt and started tearing it into sections.

"What are you doing?" Ann asked, looking up with a can of beans in her hand.

"We need rags. This shirt was getting old, anyway."

"In that big of a hurry to get naked?" Ann reached into the bag with her other hand and pulled out some paper towels. "These would probably do the trick…"

Charles paused, clutching two fistfuls of fabric. He looked down at his shirt, which was now in four pieces.

He shrugged and continued ripping. It was not like he'd be sewing it back together.

"So, these guys Tim sent, they're well trained?" Charles asked, sitting down to the table on a wobbly chair.

"Some of the best we have, actually. All are ex-Special Forces in one army or other—not all of them were American. They were elite. Been in combat zones, snuck into enemy facilities…" Ann sighed and shook her head. "They just cut out one day."

"Huh. So they got captured and you thought: they're idiots. I'm *way* better at sabotage and spy games. I think I'll go next."

"No. I thought: Sasha's bodyguards are idiots. I think I'll take a mission as far away from them as possible. Joke's on me."

"I'll say. Wait until I tell Jonas what you said about him."

Ann opened the cans before dumping the soup contents into a pot. She rested the pot on the burner and then lit it with a match.

"Camp often?" Charles asked, watching her for lack of anything better to do.

"Yes. I love camping. Which you should expect as I turn into a furry creature that lives in the mountains." She glanced over, her eyes snagging on his chest for a little too long, before looking back down at her task with a light scowl. "Shouldn't you be planning our route for tomorrow?"

"Yes. First I thought I would watch your ass, though."

"Cute."

"Yup, it is. Do you like things put in it?"

Ann scoffed, her scowl becoming more pronounced. Charles smirked and bent to the map.

∽

Ann helped Charles finish the dishes and put them on the rack before taking a large breath. Her gaze settled on the full-sized bed then looked at the large man entering the bathroom with a gloriously muscular back and broad shoulders.

He'd take up that whole bed. There wasn't a couch or even extra blankets to sleep on the floor. Just a ridiculously handsome, large man, a small bed, and her.

She sighed, moving to her duffle bag.

She slipped into a tank top as he came into the room. He froze, his eyes immediately on her disappearing breasts. She smiled to herself as she stripped out of her jeans and pulled on some small shorts. At least it wouldn't be easy for him, either. It was a tiny consolation.

She slid between the sheets and immediately sneezed as dust sifted into the air. Charles stepped forward quickly and pulled the outer layer off, leaving only a sheet and a light blanket.

"We'll be fine—you sleep hot." He still wasn't wearing a shirt after sacrificing his like a lunatic, so he stripped out of his pants, leaving him in a pair of boxers. His large erection poked out of the hole.

Her mouth went dry.

She yanked her gaze to the ceiling. "What does that mean, I sleep hot?"

"You shed body heat. You're warm. I am, too, so we don't need that outer blanket. We'll be fine."

"Okay." She cleared her throat before willing moisture back into her mouth. "I should know the answer to this, but doesn't exposing a raging hard-on bother you?"

"Why would it? It does the talking for me. I want to screw you. Now you know. So let's get to it." He slid into the covers until his body was firmly pressed up against her. His hard length pushed against her hip.

A grin tickled her lips as her core tingled. "Nah. Not interested."

"No problem. I can get you interested." His hand slid up her thigh and over her hip before rubbing across her stomach. She closed her eyes and exhaled, the feeling heavenly. His fingertips glanced the base of her breasts, but he didn't engage. Not only that, but he was staying on the surface of her clothes. He was enticing her, but not pressuring her.

That made him that much hotter and much harder to say no to.

Her body heated up and her blood boiled. She couldn't control her panting. In a wispy voice, she managed, "No thanks."

"How about a blowjob?" He nuzzled her neck, kissing her softly, raising her small hairs as shivers coated her body.

"Not in the mood."

A wet, warm tongue tickled the spot where he'd bit her.

She really wanted him to bite her again. It was so erotic, and felt so good.

"Does it feel good to you when someone takes your blood?" she asked, doing everything in her power not to spread her legs and direct his fingers to the sweet spot.

"Very. Very, very good. We don't do it often because we boost the other person's power—or, at least, I would generally boost someone else's power."

"Do I boost your power?"

His hand moved over the swell of her breast. She moaned as he kneaded lightly. "Yes. I'm the first that has taken shifter blood as far as I know. We had no idea it would, but it does. Somehow, it changes my magic a little. Incorporates yours."

"What would happen if I took your blood?"

His mouth lightly sucked at her neck. "Do you want to find out?"

She let her head fall slowly, her cheek glancing across his mouth before her lips softly touched his. He leaned forward enough to connect, the kiss turning deep and sensual almost immediately. His erection pulsed against her, begging her to turn toward him. Begging admittance.

And his mouth. The man had a gift with that mouth. Kissing, nipping, licking—he could do no wrong with it.

She wanted more, though. She wanted all of him. And if she tormented herself with just having him physically, eventually it would do exactly as Sasha warned it would. The pain of not being able to have him, or seeing him with another, would break her in half. She couldn't keep up the intimacy if she expected to be able to walk away. She was in a great place right now, more sex would blow it.

"No." Her voice came out as a breathy sigh. Talk about mixed messages.

She cleared her throat to say no with more conviction when his hand moved off her breast. It took everything she had not to snuggle in a little closer with gratitude for him understanding and not pushing the issue.

"I'm sorry, I don't want this, Charles." She laid her hand on his, which was resting on her stomach. "I don't want sex."

"We're back to the vulnerable place, I see. No problem. I'll wait until the evening when you go surly again."

She gave a soft laugh, thankful he not only understood, but that he was turning it into a joke.

He kissed her neck lightly. "Just to be clear, are blowjobs out of the question?"

She laughed again, feeling that delicious length searing against her bare skin. Her sex swelled, remembering him inside of her. Her mouth salivated at the thought of giving him pleasure.

"Yes. Out of the question, yes." It was the first time she really wanted to, though. The first time she wanted to fall to her knees in front of him and take his most precious body part into her mouth and render him speechless. Before, she had liked foreplay for mutual benefit, but now, she wanted to command him. She wanted to be the one making *him* beg.

"Prude. Fine, I'm going to jack off, because blue-balls suck. Should I go to the bathroom, outside, or do you want to get sticky?"

"Oh my God!" she laughed. "Not sticky. Gross!"

With a chuckle he rolled away from her and out of the bed. He still didn't bother to tuck himself into his boxers. "I'm going outside. If you take care of yourself, don't do it in the bed, otherwise I'll just get hard again when I come back."

"I knew you were honest, but... Jesus." Ann laughed harder, climbing out of the bed and heading to the bathroom.

Charles stepped outside with a smile and lowered his boxers, letting his dick bob out. He took it in his hand as he walked around the car, doing what Ann had done earlier and taking in the scents. He didn't smell whatever she did, though. Nothing sweet. All that registered with him was the fresh pine of the trees.

As he began stroking, he closed his eyes, letting his magic roll out around him even though there was no way he'd find anything within his range. They were dealing with either shifters or humans, not his own kind. He couldn't be positive about that, but since the Council hadn't heard anything, the neighboring clan hadn't heard anything, and neither had the Boss, he was pretty sure. Not even the clever Europeans could boast that level of secrecy.

He felt his ardor rise as a soft moan drifted out onto the breeze. The window was open in the bathroom where Ann was pleasuring herself.

A surge of heat infused him, making each stroke feel like it burned in the very best of ways. He remembered the feel of her body, and the softness of her skin. As his heart hammered in his ears, nearly there, reaching for the end, he barely registered a crack sounding in the trees.

Pleasure fired in his body, but his attention split, focusing on the world around him. It was one of his many talents.

Another crack and rustle sounded off to the distant right. Something was definitely out there.

He sampled the scents again.

There, lightly nestled between the pine, floated the distinct smell of a shifter.

With the hand not employed, he sucked his finger and put it up to the air, feeling the breeze blowing toward him. He'd heard one, but it was hard to tell if that was who he was smelling.

Pleasure forgotten, Charles walked toward the possible threat, pausing at the tree line. There was no telling how many there were. If he took off after this one, it left Ann vulnerable. She was strong and capable, but if she were outnumbered, it wouldn't matter.

He backtracked, squinting through the gaps in trees to try and minimize the glare of the sun in his eyes, looking for the disturbance.

A rustle sounded off again in the same place as before. Charles put up a hand to block the sun as another moan drifted on the breeze. Without warning, the small hairs rose on his neck and arms followed swiftly by a surge of magic. He didn't like someone else hearing Ann at such a private moment. She'd be embarrassed.

Flexing, feeling an unspeakable, protective rage well up in him, he walked backwards, closer to her. He stopped in front of the door, his tattoos swirling with magic, as he stared out at the woods in challenge. Whoever was out there, no matter how many, might be predatory animals now but they'd stemmed from humans originally—they had a soft side. In contrast, he was made to be a predator—that was what separated him from the human fork of nature. And he would protect his own like nothing that shifter out there had ever seen before.

As if hearing his thoughts, or possibly able to see him and reading his face and body language, the creature took off as if it was running for its life. Bushes and leaves rustled, rocks flew—Charles saw a brown body dash off to the right before cutting left, heading up the mountain, no bigger than a medium-sized dog. Nothing else moved.

Charles waited, his senses on alert. Nothing else moved.

There had only been one. On this side of the cabin, anyway.

There were shifters in this wood that hadn't been caught, and had not been sent by Tim. That might be cause for alarm.

CHAPTER SIX

Charles entered the cabin in a rush of adrenaline. Deep, burnished gold swirled around his arms. Magic crackled within the small space.

Ann came out of the bathroom with a sheen of sweat on her rosy face, eyes wide. "What's wrong?"

"Just saw a shifter." He flicked the deadbolt on the door and stalked to the bathroom, slamming the window shut and latching it. Back in the main room, he stared out of the window near the door, knowing he needed to lay magical tripwires of some sort. He flicked through possible spells in his head.

"A shifter?" Ann said with an incredulous voice. "What kind?"

"I only saw a flash, but it was brown and the size of a medium-sized dog."

Ann looked out the window next to him, her shifter magic swirling around her. "Think he's gone far? I could try and catch—"

"No." Charles put an arm out, backing her away from the window. "This isn't the typical war zone. This place is a danger to you. Until we know what's out there, there is no way you're running off on your own. Do you know anyone that fits that description?"

Ann looked down at her feet in thought. "A few, yeah, but they're not soldiers. None of them came up here."

"What animal could be that size and pose a threat to the group Tim sent before us?"

She shook her head. "None. Only a Tim-type animal, an alpha, would be a threat to those guys. That, or a group. You think this place is run by shifters?"

Charles slowly moved his head from side to side. "I can't think how. The brief picture we got was of a huge facility. They have high tech, and that means they have money. There aren't enough shifters to populate such a big place. There aren't enough of my kind, either. That shifter is either on patrol and working for these people, or here to check things out."

"Tim would know if someone was checking things out. He runs a tight ship with all the other packs."

Charles let the confused scowl settle over his features. "Why would a shifter work for a lab who makes shifters disappear?"

"Could be a guard to keep things quiet. Someone being as secretive as you just said wouldn't want anyone sniffing around."

"Except there've been no records of humans going missing up here. There are plenty of hikers, and cabins like this one..."

"We can speculate all day, but we won't know anything for certain until we check it out tonight."

She was right. "All right fine, then go away. You smell like sex and I want to climb on. I can't be distracted when I try to work magic or something will get messed up."

"Do you blow things up?"

"No, that's a Sasha and Paulie thing. Well, I guess any human trained wrong. If we—Go away. Your chatter isn't helping. I can still smell you."

"Prickly." Ann moved off toward the bed and slipped in, propping herself up on an elbow to watch him.

He could still smell the aroma of her climax, not to mention her normal mouth-watering scent. It lingered in the air like a delicious beacon. The sheets were settled at her waist, giving a great view of those perky breasts through the tank top...

Charles squeezed his eyes shut to block out her image. "This would be a whole lot easier if you'd just let me screw you real quick."

"I can imagine."

"If you could imagine, you'd spread your legs and wave me in." Charles took a deep breath and focused on the area outside the window. "Okay. Here goes."

He pulled the elements and mixed them just right, using mostly earth to root the spell and water for its substance. If he set it right, if someone tripped the spell with their physical presence, he'd be alerted. Nothing more. He could then at least assess what was trying to sneak up on him.

Once the spell was formed, he spread it out in front of the cabin, just beyond his SUV. That done, he moved to the other sides of the cabin, laying out similar spells. Unlike Sasha and Paulie, he wasn't good enough to do it all at once, but this would work, too.

A solid sweat stood out on his brow from the effort by the time he had finished. He returned to his initial position and laid a simpler spell for any magic that crossed the threshold. The principle would be the same as the other—alerting, not attacking.

Finally, he fell into the bed next to Ann. "I hate doing that stuff. It takes so much energy."

"But we'll know if they try to sneak up on us?"

"Hopefully. Then we can decide what to do. I didn't want to try an attack spell because I'd probably do something wrong."

"And it would probably only get one person. If there was anyone else, they'd know what they were up against." Ann curled up next to his side. "I'm cold. Can I have some body heat without having to give anything for it?"

Charles lifted his arm so she could scoot closer. She put a hand across his middle and a leg over his as her head found the hollow between his neck and his shoulder. She sighed in contentment as his arm came around her, squeezing her closer.

"I won't let anything happen to you, Ann. No matter what happens, I won't let anyone hurt you."

Her arm tightened for a moment before sliding up his chest and hooking around his neck.

He hoped to hell he could make good on his word.

∼

As the evening rolled through, sapping out all the light from the day, Charles and Ann found themselves stalking through the trees near the top of the mountain. They'd taken the SUV up the main road for a while before stashing it, then continuing on foot.

Ann had wanted to change into her animal form to make the journey easier, but Charles had talked her out of it. There was something about this whole situation that meant the least amount of shifter attributes she used, the better.

"*God* it smells good up here." Ann took a huge breath. Her eyes glazed over for a moment as a dopey smile plastered her face.

Charles' brow furrowed as he tried to smell what she did.

All he got was pine, the soft scent of mulch, and Ann's comforting and erotic smell. Nothing else, and certainly nothing that would make his eyes glaze over.

"Where's it coming from?" he asked, surveying what lay in front of them.

They were about a hundred yards from the fence that enclosed the large facility according to the map. And though the trees weren't especially dense, there were a lot of them between where they were and their goal. Visibility was minimal.

"That way." Ann pointed in front of her before she wiped drool from the side of her mouth.

"Catnip for shifters in the air?" Charles asked in thought as he scanned the ground. A smallish paw print etched the dirt lightly. It could've been a dog. It could've been a shifter.

"Sounds unlikely."

"Yes. It does. Yet, every time you take a deep breath, you get all... hazy-eyed." Charles stalked closer silently, monitoring the ground for traps or pitfalls. His magic coated the ground in front of him, sensing for magic or anything out of the ordinary.

Fifty yards along, he finally caught a glimpse of what they were after. He pulled out his phone as Ann bumped into him. She stumbled beside him and sat down roughly, staring with a confused expression.

Warning bled into Charles. "What's wrong?" He rested a hand on her shoulder.

She barely acknowledged his touch. "I don't know. I'm just... light-headed. That *smell*."

"Stay put, then, okay? I'm going to go a bit closer. If something happens, run back to the cabin and call for backup. Don't try to help."

"Don't think I could help. I don't know what's happening to me, Charles." Her voice had become a plea for help. "I feel... really good. But... like I'm not in my body. Maybe it's an airborne drug or something. Like a gas that's aimed to affect shifters."

"Probably." Charles brushed her hair back from her face, feeling his chest pinch at the sight of her glassy stare, almost devoid of the sharp intelligence he was used to seeing in her eyes. "Okay, just stay put. I'm going to get a few pictures."

"'Kay."

Uncomfortable with leaving her alone, but seeing no alternative, Charles snuck closer to the fence, keeping his magic wrapped firmly around him. He would be mostly masked from humans with the shadows clinging to his body, and also from uneducated shifters. Tim's crew could pick up Charles' kind, even deep in the shadows, but they relied more on their senses than eyes. Unsuspecting shifters probably wouldn't.

Hopefully wouldn't.

He approached the fence, snapping off pictures with his phone, though he had no service. He'd have to call the Boss from the cabin.

The fence was a standard affair, about eight feet tall with barbed wire curled along the top. Signs every so often promised electrocution if someone touched the shiny metal. On the other side, loose dirt covered a large open area with a plethora of dog or shifter tracks. A few feet away lay a loose cluster of, what he assumed, was dog poop. He was pretty sure shifters used toilets, no matter what Jonas claimed. He caught whiffs of urine, no doubt from the same animals that patrolled, marking their territory.

Another fifty yards away stood the side of a single-story building, dotted with windows, and a single door to the right. The structure had no embellishments of architectural design; it was a solid, concrete building dominating the natural landscape.

As Charles snapped off pictures, a lone animal came trotting along the fence. Sleek and mostly black, it was a dog with pointed ears. Doberman.

It came closer, its nose twitching. A low whine started in its throat that quickly turned into a growl. It stopped ten feet from him, staring in his direction and baring its teeth.

"Shoo!" Charles whispered furiously. He sent a light, magical shock toward the animal. The dog yelped and jumped backward. The growl grew louder.

"Oh, you have courage, do you?" Charles took its picture before sending a harder shock. The dog yelped again, and jogged back a few paces before barking.

Damn dog.

Charles backed away from the fence. He had what he came for, anyway.

The dog barked again.

"I'm leaving, for cripes-sakes!" Charles muttered, backing away quicker. He didn't want to kill the thing, but if it didn't bugger off and mind its own business soon, he'd probably have to.

Maybe Sasha knew some non-fatal tricks for dealing with dogs.

He backtracked through the trees until he reached his starting point. Ann was gone.

"Fuck." Heart pounding, he bent to the ground. He saw her butt print, and then a mess of disturbed dirt and mulch from when she must've staggered up. Her footprints led away at a diagonal toward the fence. Usually she stepped in a precise way, graceful and light on her feet, but here her prints were sloppy, as though she was half-stumbling.

Adrenaline coursed through his body as a nervous sweat broke out on his forehead. With a tight chest and barely contained panic, he followed the trail, hating himself that he had left her behind. She'd seemed fine to sit. Hazy, but not totally gone.

Maybe whatever was in the air had a compound effect...

The tracks veered right before a disturbance in the dirt showed them going left again. Definitely staggering, as though she were drunk.

He heard a soft shuffle ahead. The rustle of branches.

Charles started to jog, and saw swinging branches and raining needles before seeing Ann's shape falter, almost at the fence.

"Ann! Stop!" Charles put on a burst of speed, jamming his phone into his pocket.

Slowing, looking around confusedly, she put out her hands as though blind and feeling her way. "Charles?" she asked in a small voice.

She staggered forward a few more feet, stopping in a cleared area in front of a gate. "Charles?"

"Hang on, Ann. I'm right here."

He was five feet away when she took one more step toward the gate.

The sound of twisting metal rang out. Something snapped with a *clang*. Like a metallic blanket, a large net sprung up from the ground. The trap closed around Ann's body, cinched tight at the top and connected to a hook. A cable went taut, dragging the net toward a tree a few feet away.

With his heart in his throat, Charles whipped out his sword. The cable looped through a pulley in the tree before running back to the ground where a motorized winch turned, dragging the net into the air.

"What's... happening?" Forced to curl into a ball, Ann's little hand curled around one of the metal cables of her prison.

"Don't worry, I've got it." Charles rushed to the side, sword glowing with magic. He swung with all his might, not sure if his magic would cut through metal. The blade bounced off, jarring his shoulder, but leaving a slash mark in the cable. He threaded more fire into his weapon and swung again, using all his strength. The blade bit deeper this time, slicing.

A door opened to his right—someone was coming out of the building.

Without a moment to lose, he slashed again. The dull clink of magical metal on cable sounded before the net fell to the ground.

"Hey!" someone shouted.

"Hurry, Ann!" Charles rushed to the net where Ann was struggling like someone in deep water who couldn't swim. "C'mon baby. Let's get you out of there."

He sheathed his sword to use both hands, ripping at the net where it attached to the hook. The magic helped peel away the material.

A motor became active, shuddering the gate to life. It began to open slowly with two large men in gray uniforms waiting patiently. A dog waited with him.

"Hurry!" Charles ripped the last of the net away, bending in to grab Ann around the waist and haul her out. He could easily kill those humans and the dog, even if the dog was actually a shifter, but then the entire facility would know that something mean and dangerous had showed up on their doorstep. He didn't need that kind of attention. Not yet, anyway.

Throwing Ann over his shoulder, he took off at a run, dodging through the trees toward his car. Barking sounded off behind him, the dog freed from the confines of its yard and in pursuit.

He put on a burst of speed. As the car came into sight, he heard the rough panting of an animal gaining on them.

He swung, dropping Ann gently to the ground before facing the attacker. The dog was there a moment later, trained to chase and jump for the jugular. Charles waited until the animal was mid-leap, teeth flashing, before grabbing the beast out of the air and punching it in the side.

The animal bayed in pain as Charles threw it to the ground. He punched the dog's head next, knocking it out.

Breathing heavily, he stared down at the animal just to make sure it wouldn't get up. When it didn't, he bent to put his hand on its chest. A heart beat pushed back on his palm.

It was still alive. He'd done his good deed for the night.

He turned back toward the car and saw Ann, leaning against the hood. She shook her head and blinked a few times, the clarity coming back into her eyes.

"What the hell is going on?" she asked, looking up at Charles with huge, fear-filled eyes.

"They have something that confuses shifters. C'mon, let's go back to the cabin and call the Boss. We need to get smart people in on this."

"I'd make a joke, but I still can't think clearly."

"That's okay." Charles opened the passenger-side door before scooping her up into his arms. "Your jokes are terrible, anyway."

He put her into the seat before buckling her in and closing the door. When he had slid into the driver's side, she said, "After what just happened, I think a car accident is the least of our worries."

"Which is why it'll probably happen, just to spite me." Charles pulled out and headed back to the cabin. "I might try to work out some attack spells. We aren't going to be safe at that cabin. A shifter getting out of a trap raises a lot of questions. They'll know you had help, or they'll think it was a human who got caught. That net is a danger to humans. It would also raise questions about their facility, not to mention bring on a lawsuit. Either way, that crowd won't be thrilled about unanswered questions…"

"*I'm* not thrilled with unanswered questions."

Charles pulled up close to the cabin, and then walked around to help Ann out. She faltered a little, resting her hand on his arm for support, but her eyes looked much clearer.

"What did it feel like?" Charles asked as he helped her inside and locked the door behind them. He went to the sink to get her a glass of water.

She sat on the bed, holding her head in her hands. "At first, like I was high. I hate drugs because I hate the feeling of not being able to think straight. That was exactly what it felt like in the beginning. I could work through that at first, but then it got stronger. I got distracted really easily. I just couldn't think, then I couldn't control myself. It was like I was a passenger in my own body. Before I knew it, I was walking. When I realized it, and tried to come back, I just kept stumbling." She looked up at him, the pleading back in her eyes. "It almost reminded me of when I first changed. All the hormones, and the magic, and the inner-struggles. Changing messes with your head in the beginning. So it was like that, but after a bunch of bong rips."

"It's targeted toward shifters, I think we can agree on that. Maybe they've figured out your hormone mix when you first shift, and concocted something to target those areas in your brain. Or something."

"Did you feel it at all?"

Charles sat next to her, his phone in his hand. She leaned against his shoulder and he put his arm around her, pulling her close, feeling her trembling against him. What had happened had really thrown her. She wasn't used to not being in control, and apparently the walk down memory lane to a confusing and traumatizing time had put her off her game.

"No. I didn't smell or feel anything," Charles answered, rubbing her arm.

"I thought with my blood..."

He shook his head. It was a reasonable thought, and he was thankful it hadn't come to pass.

"Maybe if I took your blood, it would help?" she asked in a tiny voice.

A thrill went through him, making his heart speed up and a hard-on start. "I've taken a lot of your blood in the last two days. If you take some of mine, it might initiate a blood link. It would in humans, anyway. Not sure with shifters."

"Maybe that would be good, though? You know… just in case."

Charles could hear the fear in her voice. She'd almost been caught by a group of people who knew how to ensnare shifters. Who knew enough about the genetic makeup of shifters to concoct something that *could* ensnare them. That was not a good sign, especially as Tim already thought the facility was a lab of some sort.

Charles blew out a breath. "We'd be tied forever, Ann. Lightly, maybe, if we stopped swapping blood after, but it would always be there. When you find a guy to settle down with and have kitties, I'll be a silent passenger. I don't think you want that."

"I'd rather that than a cage and getting experimented on."

"But my blood might not prevent that."

"It would help you find me if I got caught."

Charles gritted his teeth at the soft vulnerability in her voice. At the desire to throw her back right there and take her.

What he hadn't said was that he worried *he'd* be the one regretting it. He didn't want to see her find someone else. He didn't want to see her settling down with some loser fox, or whatever, and popping out a bunch of furry babies. He wanted her as she had been: a pain in his ass, making fun of him and playing jokes. He wanted her as she had been yesterday: more than willing to share his bed, giving and receiving explosive orgasms then being totally fine with falling asleep by his side.

Why couldn't she be cool with his lifestyle? He'd give her kids if he could. He'd give her a family. He'd even live in the same place and leave his heart with her, because now he knew that there was something there besides just friendship. He cared about her more than anyone else. He had for a long time, if he was completely honest with himself.

He just didn't want to go all in. It wasn't what his people did. It wasn't the way things were.

Charles stood up in a rush, conflicted. "You make my life hell."

She snorted, clasping her hands in her lap. "It's more fun than taking up stenciling."

He walked to the window and looked out, half expecting to see people sneaking up on them. "I need to fortify those spells, and then I'm going to call the Boss."

"I need to call Tim. It would've been easier if Tim and Stefan were in the same place, especially since I don't have much to tell."

"The Boss will sort it out. Hopefully he'll tell us to pull out. Otherwise, we're going to have company."

CHAPTER SEVEN

Ann hit "end" and stared out the window for a moment, reflecting on the call with Tim. She'd explained what had happened, what she'd experienced, and that she'd been rescued by Charles. There wasn't any point in trying to cover up the fact that if it hadn't been for Charles, she'd most likely be inside that facility with everyone else.

Admitting the truth had been made easier, of course, by Charles' complete lack of ego regarding his role in the situation. He didn't place any blame, point any fingers, or adopt any swagger. He acted exactly the same in this as he always had when defending Sasha. He took care of business.

Sasha knew how lucky she was getting him as a bodyguard, but it was the first time Ann was a bit jealous.

"It'd be better with Paulie up here, then," Charles said into the phone as he braced his muscular arm on the window pane. He listened for a second, his tone respectfully argumentative. "She can't function when she breathes that stuff in, though. She goes wandering off. None of the shifters would be good in this situation..."

The only consolation to Ann's failure was that it wasn't

specific to her. Whatever was going on in that facility, they'd figured out a special formula that could affect her kind.

A tremor of fear worked through her.

For that kind of knowledge, they must have experimented on shifters, and those experiments would probably have been invasive. She had a lot of courage, but if she was unable to protect herself, the smart thing to do would be to get the hell away from the problem.

Unfortunately, then she'd be letting Tim down. She'd volunteered for this duty, and failure would make her look like an idiot.

"One more day, but then I have to call it." Charles' voice took on an edgy quality Ann rarely heard from him. "I'll get a few more pictures, and then we're coming back. Seriously, Jameson, there's no point in toting her, or any shifter, around behind us. They get all weird by that stuff. To get a look inside, we need a few of our kind—or even humans— with a good magical disguise. If we wait too long, they'll probably figure us out too, and then we're fucked."

Ann moved to the kitchen and started picking out cans for dinner.

"Fine. Put Sasha on—I need some nasty magical traps to lay."

Ann got busy making a meal while Charles laid whatever spells Sasha was trying to walk him through. Then something occurred to her.

When Charles got off the phone, shaking with fatigue from working the spells, she placed steaming bowls on the table. "If they had a shifter running around yesterday, how come he didn't get pulled in by the smell?" she asked.

Charles plopped into the chair with a sigh. "If they're smart enough to come up with something that affects shifters like it does, I'm sure they have an antidote. Or maybe he was a rogue shifter who won't be bothering us again."

Charles scooped some chili up. "I have some nasty things set around here." He chewed for a moment. "Sasha dumbed down her spells, but she had to get creative. She's been trained too well by Toa. The enemy will get a nasty surprise, that's for sure."

"Which will probably start a war between that facility and us."

"Yup, but we have no choice if we want to stay safe. Tomorrow we're going to snap off a few more pictures, try to get the front of the place, then leave. Jameson wants to plan how to get inside and see what's going on. The question is: leave you here, or take you with me..."

"If I go, I'll probably just be in the way."

"And if you stay, you probably won't be here when I get back."

"There's that. I can just take the car down the hill and wait."

Charles scooped a spoonful into his mouth as he stared at her, his smoky-gray eyes troubled. "I'm sure they have vehicles. I'm not sure they would follow you, but... I just don't know, Ann. This is a bad situation."

"Let's just go snap off some pictures now. Tonight. Then we're out of here."

He nodded as he scooped another mouthful. "I thought of that. We could, but they'll be roused. We only have a few hours before daylight. There are bound to be more people around the facility in the day, not to mention the lack of shadows for me to hide in. Humans are stupid, but a big guy in plain daylight they would notice. Probably."

"I feel like baggage." Ann ate her chili regardless of her lack of appetite.

"You look like an old bag."

"Nice."

Charles grinned as he finished off his bowl. "Is this all we have? Because I'm still hungry. Also, all this danger has made me horny. You ready to screw yet, or what?"

"I'll screw you if you give me blood." Ann shook her head at herself as she got up to dump another can into the pot. "What is wrong with me? I can't *believe* I just said that."

"So... just screw? No blood?"

She slowed down her movements, thinking.

Something in her said his blood, and that link, was a safety net she couldn't do without. A heavy weight in her gut was a warning that there was a good chance she'd be taken. Either tonight or tomorrow sometime, they'd find her and drag her away. Charles was vicious and an excellent fighter when he had to be, but he was just one. And they probably had guns.

The question was, did she want to be tied with him forever?

Yes, she did. But would she still want to be once she'd found someone else and started a life?

Probably not, but it was impossible to think that far ahead, especially with the danger in front of her.

She sighed and went back to her bowl, leaving the stirring spoon on the counter. "You can take it from there."

Charles frowned at her before getting up to stir the pot. "I was having a nice time being lazy and getting waited on."

"Uh huh. Fascinating."

She ate slowly, finishing at about the time Charles finished his second portion. By the way he glanced at the store of cans, he was thinking about a third. The man could eat.

She washed her bowl and put it in the rack as he came up behind her. She stalled at the sink, hoping he would wrap his arms around her. When he didn't, she washed her hands and finished up.

"Get a move on, varmint. You take forever at this domestic stuff."

She smiled as she turned toward him and wiped her wet hands on his shirt.

"*Ah*, c'mon! This is a new shirt."

Laughing, she finished drying her hands and walked to her duffle, taking out a book. They had nothing to do but wait and sleep. She might as well try to distract herself.

Charles came over a few minutes later. He reached in his bag and took out a strip of putrid brown knitting with a ball of yarn attached to it. He settled onto the bed next to her, knitting needles at the ready.

"That is... terrible." Ann flicked the ball of yarn. "What are you making, a knitted log of dog poop?"

"That's just hurtful."

"Charles! That is the exact color of poop. Or one of the colors, anyway. One of the grosser varieties. Why in the world are you making something out of it?"

His needles started working, tick-ticking in the quiet room.

"What happened to the pink... wrap... thing?" she tried.

"That's on hold. I figured I'd make this for you, first."

"For me?" She stared incredulously at the horrible brown yarn. "Why?"

"I happen to know you never throw away a thoughtful present. You even wear said thoughtful present at least once. And since you made fun of the wrap, I thought you might need something knitted for you. Like a hat. That everyone will see when you wear it."

"And the color?"

"Is really ugly." He grinned as his needles worked even faster. "You're welcome."

She had to hand it to him, he could really move those knitting needles. Too bad he picked weird designs and hideous colors...

"What are you reading?" he asked, glancing over.

She showed him the cover of the book, featuring a bare man-chest with a wolf in the background.

"Ah. Women's fantasy, huh? Reading about the perfect guy?" He smirked as he glanced out the window, not needing to look at his hands while he was employed. "Read to me. We can role play the sex scenes."

"How do you know it has sex scenes?"

The needles stopped for a moment. He looked at her with one raised eyebrow.

She smirked with a red face, looking down at her book. "Okay, fine, it has sex scenes. It also has shifters—werewolves. I get a kick out of how wrong they get our kind."

The tick-ticking started again.

"Read to me. I like hearing about sex if I can't have it," Charles pushed.

"I'm not going to read to you. They are having a heart-to-heart about his damaged past at the moment. You'll just laugh."

"I also like comedy. Those books have it all. C'mon." He nudged her with his elbow. "I'm bored. I don't need to really focus to knit—it's just something to occupy my hands while I wait for stuff. It's calming."

Ann gave a loud sigh, unable to help the smile, nor the red face. "Fine." She looked through the page, finding the paragraph she'd left off, when Charles' body went rigid. His muscles flexed. The room fell into silence as the needles stopped.

Ann looked up as Charles' eyes went distant. His arms flared with color.

"What?" Ann whispered, her stomach churning with what she suspected.

Charles jumped off the bed. "Turn off that light."

Ann dove for the camping lantern next to the bed, flicking it off as Charles reached the window. He leaned against the side, peeking out. Ann went to the window across from him, doing the same thing.

"Did they cross?" she asked as her gaze scanned the still and looming trees outside.

"One triggered. It was a tamer spell—like a bunch of mosquitoes all biting at once. Nothing else has been disturbed."

"It was over there?"

"On this side, yes."

Ann's stomach flipped. "Was it close to the car?"

Charles looked at her, the moonlight lighting half of his handsome face. "Yes. Why?"

"Did you cover your license plate?"

Charles sighed as he looked back out the window. "Doesn't have one yet—the car is brand new. They can't track me that way."

Ann met his sigh. "That's probably what they were after, though. Probably wanted to have a look in the car, and maybe the cabin, too. Are you feeling with your magic right now?"

"Yes, but I don't feel anything. I don't have much range, though."

They held their positions for what felt like hours, waiting in silence.

"I wonder if they know what that magic is," Ann wondered quietly. "If they know what you are."

Charles looked her way again.

"I had no idea of your kind before the Council approached us," she elaborated. "It wasn't something anyone talked about. There are still people in Tim's various packs that don't know about you. His immediate one does, sure, because we work with you. But a lot of your clans are still hostile toward shifters, so Tim has only informed the various sub-alphas and they are keeping quiet. He hasn't told a lot of the lower ranks. You are most definitely an anomaly to humans, but probably also to the shifter around here. Don't you think?"

Charles looked back out the window. "I kind of hope I'm not, because then that shifter would know to stay away. But you're probably right. Regardless, I don't feel anything. Whatever it is, it isn't trying to get through anymore."

"Or else it's waiting and watching..."

"Now who's ruining the chi?"

Ann crossed to the bed and picked up her book. She flung it to her duffle. "I don't think a light is the best idea."

"And you need it." Charles crossed back to his side of the bed and picked up his needles and yarn again, not relaxed, but no longer tense, either.

"No. I don't need it. I can do a lot of things in the dark. Like sit here, watching you knit."

Charles huffed out a laugh and folded up his hobby. "Or sleep."

"Yeah. Actually, that's a better idea, because without heavy shades on this place, I won't be able to sleep well in the daylight. My kind is usually awake during the day."

"Uh huh. Fascinating," Charles mimicked her from earlier.

Ann rolled her eyes and stripped off her shirt and bra, bending to her duffle for a tank top to sleep in. That on, she stripped out of her pants, changed her underwear, and put on little shorts. When she turned back around, Charles was staring at her, knitting supplies still in hand. The soft moonlight streaming in the windows draped across his face, amplifying his handsomeness.

"What?" she asked.

"You have, quite possibly, the best breasts I have ever seen. They're perfect. Perfect size, perfect shape, they taste good... It's really not fair that you keep them to yourself."

"I don't intend to."

"Really?" Charles stripped off his shirt and out of his

pants so fast her mouth dropped. When he dropped his boxers, his thick erection bounced up, ready for her.

Her core heated, wanting him inside her so bad her knees got weak. Her nipples contracted with the thought, advertising her desire through her tank top.

Barely keeping her composure, she answered, "Yeah. When I find someone that likes me, I intend to share them with him every time he wants to play with them."

"I like you. And sharing is caring. So let's do this thing."

"Likes me for longer than a night. Or day, depending."

"I'll like you for many days. Over and over, too. And over."

Ann rolled her eyes and crawled into bed. "Loves me, then. When I find someone that *loves* me, I will share the breasts."

Charles slid in slowly, his gaze lifting to her eyes. The sparkle of heat had dulled, replaced with wariness. Ann's heart sank.

"Anyway." She pulled the covers up to her chin. "We should probably get some sleep. I bet you someone will turn up in the daylight. An official someone too, just checking in with the inhabitants of this cabin."

"Ann…" Charles turned on his side to face her, his body flush against hers. He ran his thumb across the base of her chin. "If you want blood, or a blood link, I'll do it. If it'll help, or ease your mind, I will do it."

Ann let her head fall so she could meet his gaze, nearly lost to the darkness. His face was so close to hers their breath mingled. Her body hummed with the proximity, feeling his delicious muscles pressed against her and his hard length against her thigh.

"I'm on the fence about it," she whispered, her eyes dipping to his shapely lips. "I want it right now, yes. I want you right now. But we both know we want different things.

Creating a tie at this moment might be really dumb for the future."

"Losing you would kill me, Ann. If you get taken somehow, and I can't find you..."

"We'll be careful."

"There's no guarantee in this place. We might not even last the day. And it'll be *you* that's taken. They seem to have 'catching shifters' down pretty well. They won't know about me until people are dead, and by then it might be too late." Charles laid his hand against her cheek. "I don't really want to feel you with anyone else, but if it means your life, and your happiness, then I'll do whatever it takes. You deserve that, and if it's in my power to give it, I will."

"Did you read this in a 'how to sweet-talk chicks' book?" She ran her hand up his arm, across his collarbone, and then down his chest, feeling the definition. A slow burn started in her sex, aching to be touched.

"No. Not this. I mean it, Ann. Whatever you need, I'll do."

She leaned forward, touching her lips to his. Electricity shocked through her body, having her opening her mouth and leaning up on an elbow, deepening the kiss. He rolled onto his back and brought his arm around her, pulling her in tight.

"Feeling you with someone else wouldn't make a happy life for me, Charles," she said softly as she leaned over his chest. Her lips just barely glanced off his, savoring the feeling of being so close. "You know that."

"I can block the link," he whispered, his hand under her tank top and lightly grazing her skin. "You won't feel me with anyone else."

"Can I block it from my end?"

He paused as a crease wormed between his eyebrows. "I don't know. You might need magic to do it. I don't know how the link would work with shifter magic."

"You might not even be able to feel me in shifter form."

"It's worth a try," he said softly. His head lifted to connect with her lips again, his kiss slow and deep.

Her hand felt his rock-hard abs before slipping down, finding the other rock-hard part of his anatomy. She stroked that velvety skin gently, hearing a low moan deep in his throat.

"How do we do it?" she asked, feeling a strange sort of excitement bubbling within her.

"It's an intimate and erotic thing, sharing blood. So when you feel it, cut my vein—or bite it if you can—and drink. Humans can have a hard time digesting blood, but we can try it and see."

"I've eaten raw animal—I can handle blood."

Charles' hand found the back of her neck, pulling her harder into the kiss. Her breath sped up, as did her hand, feeling the anticipation. Wanting the hard and fast connection of his body in hers.

He sat up in a rush, lifting her to a seated position, before ripping off her shirt. "I have no idea why that is so hot."

"What? Eating raw animal?" Ann sucked in a breath as Charles licked a taut nipple. He sucked it in, fondling the other expertly. She ran her fingers through his hair, breath speeding up.

"Hunting. Killing." Charles pushed her to the bed so he could strip off her small shorts and panties. "It's natural and primal. It's something humans don't do. It speaks directly to my primal side. It's fucking hot, Ann."

One hand on each of her inner thighs, he pushed her legs open and licked up her sex, having her gasping in sudden pleasure. He sucked her clit, twirling the nub with his tongue at the same time. Sensation started to pound at her, speeding up her heart. A finger dipped into her, then two, rubbing to compliment the sucking.

"Oh... *God,*" she breathed, running her hands up her face and clutching at her hair. "You are so good at that."

His finger worked faster as his mouth worked harder, the sensations more intense. Pulling at her middle. Breath coming out in ragged pants. She moaned, then again, loud and desperate. Her hips swung up as those fingers worked. As his mouth pleasured her.

"Oh, Charles. I'm going to—" An orgasm shook her body and chattered her teeth. She arched up, clenching and flexing, riding out the waves of pleasure.

Charles kissed up her stomach, ready to fill her body with himself.

Not this time, though.

She sat up and slid out from under him, pushing his shoulder gently. He rolled over at her unspoken command, looking up at her with eyes on fire, sparkling in the moonlight streaming through the window.

Starting slow, she gently kissed between his pecs, making the touches light and teasing. She lightly played with his nipple, knowing men liked it almost as much as women. She sucked it as her hands tickled down his stomach, flowing to the side to barely touch the edges of his pubic area.

His breath caught.

Smiling, she gave some attention to the other nipple as her fingers danced along his thighs before coming back up, passing a little closer to his balls and large erection.

"Oh," he groaned, his voice soaked with desire.

She worked her way down his deliciously bumpy stomach, so defined and cut it made her mouth water. Her fingers did another pass, even closer. His breath hitched again. His fingers twitched before grabbing the sheets on the bed. He was probably doing everything in his power not to grab fistfuls of her hair and force her head lower.

She licked down his happy trail then rose up a little,

letting the tip of her tongue touch the very tip of his erection.

"No, Ann. No. This is not—that's fucked up, Ann. Just suck on it. I don't like torture."

She clamped down on a giggle, noticing his fists pulling the sheet away from the mattress. Charles was under extreme duress.

Payback was a bitch.

She wet her lips and lightly kissed down the underside of his cock, wetness and warmth barely touching sensitive skin. At the base, she applied a little more pressure with her tongue while lightly stroking his balls. His hips rose up, forcing his erection up toward her, but she backed off.

"I hate you," he whispered, strain lacing his voice.

She couldn't stop the giggle this time.

"Chicks don't do this to dudes, Ann. We can't handle it."

"I want to hear you beg. I want repayment."

"And dudes definitely don't beg."

"Dudes, chicks—what are you, Californian?"

"Disgruntled, actually. Suck it. Just suck it down." He was almost whining. His head was pushed into the pillow with his eyes squeezed shut in discomfort. Every muscle on his body was flexed, giving her an impressive display.

She wet her lips again before taking him in one deep gulp, relaxing her throat and taking him all the way in. She sucked hard as she pulled back, taking him to that strange line between pleasure and pain, where it hurt so damn good, but where fear fired the body's pistons, not sure if adrenaline would be needed in a moment to fight the pain.

"Ohhh, *oh*... oh fu... oh ga..." Charles' arms lifted. Sheets tore away from the bed in a show of muscle.

Instead of sucking him back in, though, she lightly blew on the wetness she'd created.

"No. *No!* Oh fuck, no, please Ann. Don't do that." Charles

arched back, pulling the clutched sheets to his chest now, utterly ruining the makeup of the bedclothes and showing the dingy mattress beneath them.

She didn't need to see that last bit.

"Are you sure, Charles?" She blew again before tickling his tip with her tongue lightly. "You want me to stop?"

"Do not stop, woman."

"Then ask me nicely to suck your cock."

"Oh please. Please, please. Please suck my cock, Ann. I'll do anything. Anything you want. Want your car washed? Hair washed? Daily screws? Me dancing around in a tutu? Fucking anything. Please, Ann."

Ann had to take a moment to stare in confusion, a smile taking over her lips. *Carwash? Tutu?* She'd broken his brain.

Giggling again because of his colorful begging, but knowing that it counted as begging, she did as he asked, and sucked him in again. This time she loosened the suction as she pulled back, all pleasure. Hand at his base, other hand massaging his balls, she took him in again, starting a slow rhythm. It didn't take long for his hips to start pumping up into her, though. Needing it faster. Harder.

She increased her tempo, her hands in sync with the pumping of her mouth, taking him deep before sucking as she pulled back. She matched the pace of his hips and then sped up when he did, taking his cues.

"I'm going to come, Ann. Get ready or get out of the way!"

Ann kept going, ready and willing. He gave a loud, long moan, signaling his release. She took him down easy, easing up as his muscles started to unclench. After a quick wipe with the back of her hand, she kissed his stomach softly, working up his body, aiming for his neck.

She was going to do it. She was going to establish a connection with him that would never go away.

Oh God, she was nervous.

She settled over his body and lightly kissed up the vulnerable, soft skin. She licked over his hot pulse.

"Are you ready?" she asked in a breathy voice.

"I should be inside you when we do this. It feels better that way."

"Can you get hard again?"

Charles tsked. "Who the hell are you talking to—*can I get hard again?* I am the man with the magical dick! I can always get hard again. It might kill me after that fucking awesome blowjob, which should win an award by the way, but yeah, I can handle this. Just give me a minute."

Smiling into his neck, she kissed him softly and moved her wetness over his manhood slowly, helping him back to life.

"Kiss me, baby" Charles commanded softly.

Goosebumps raced across her skin with the term of endearment. But she didn't move up that way. She knew how weird guys were about swallowing and then deep kissing. Not that she blamed them, entirely. That stuff was not awesome.

"Should I brush my teeth?" she asked quietly, running her hands up his arms as she laid on his chest.

"I've been in the trenches. Not really my cup of tea, but it can really harden you, that's for sure. Come up here."

Ann shook her head with a smile, lifting so that she rested her lips over his.

"Besides, complaining when you went above and beyond is ungrateful." He kissed her lips, running his hands up her back. "I really care about you, Ann. You are one of my favorite people."

"You aren't one of mine. I'm just after your body," Ann whispered, kissing down his neck again.

"Join the club." Charles pushed upward before pulling his

hips back, rubbing his length against her wetness. "Hmmm, that's better. Not long now."

Ann's eyes drifted closed and her head sank, her cheek resting against his, as the sensation spiraled through her body. "Don't you get tired of sex without feeling?"

Charles stilled for a moment, his body tensing slightly. "Yes. I was at that point before you seduced me. Just... bored."

"Seduced you? I flat out told you I wanted to screw you."

"I know. Seduced me."

"So you have a new lay for now. What'll happen when you get bored again?"

Charles shifted his upper body, leaning away from her kisses. He didn't take his cock away from her sex though. Clearly there were limits to how far he was willing to go to get away from an uncomfortable conversation.

"Honestly... I don't think I will. I mean, I might, but it'll take a while, because you give great head, and you have great breasts, you're uncommonly beautiful, and you're a real bitch, which I like. It'll take a long time to get bored of you..."

"Such sweet words. Shakespeare's got nothing on you."

"I know. I study." Charles shifted back, moving close again. "I could give you most of what you're after, Ann. I know you want kids and a stable man and a house—I can give you all that."

"You'd have sex with some other woman, and then come home with her sweat and kisses on your body." Ann shivered, pain seeping into her. "To me, that says you want someone else. That I'm not good enough. It's a cultural thing. I know that you can separate family from dick swinging, as Jonas calls it, and that almost your entire culture does it. But I can't. It would kill me to know you want to be with someone else."

"Sasha once zapped a female who got too close to the

Boss. She was about to do worse, but I stopped her. I get it, I just..."

"Don't want to be castrated by it."

"Yikes." Charles shivered. "I was going to say imprisoned. You're a scary bitch. Which I also like."

Charles angled her face to his and kissed her, deep and sensual. He ran his hardness up her sex again before reaching down to cup her butt. He angled up, reaching between them to guide himself into her opening. "Your possessiveness turns me on."

Ann sighed as he filled her, then winced. "Be gentle. I'm sore."

"And so damn tight." Charles entered her mouth with his tongue, holding himself deep in her body.

"I wasn't being possessive, I was telling you I couldn't share you."

"Then used the word castration. Hmm, Ann. Sassy." He held her tightly to his chest and pulled out slowly, before just as slowly, pushing back in again.

The topical pain made her wince even as the deeper pleasure had her eyes fluttering. He worked slowly, overcoming her body's protests little by little. When the pain had begun to subside, and things were starting to heat up, Ann pushed herself up and astride him.

"Okay, so..." She rocked her hips forward, feeling his girth rub against her insides *just right*. "We do this until the need to suck on your neck overcomes me?"

Charles braced his hands on her hips, held her firmly, and then pumped up into her. Their bodies met with a sinful *smack*.

"Oh God," she breathed, rolling her hips in a circle. He did it again, pumping into her with a hard thrust.

"Oh..." She started gyrating on top of him, letting him lift her and pull her back down as he thrust upwards. Her movements had him hitting all the right places as he jarred the pleasure deeper.

Her motions became frantic. His thrusts grew more intense.

"When you get near orgasm, take it then," he panted, *thrusting* upward.

"Will you... take more... of mine?"

"That'd make the connection deeper. So only if you want to."

Ann's eyes fluttered as she leaned forward, bracing her hands on his pecs. Eyes closed, pleasure soaking up into her body, she whispered, "I want to."

"Then you can take my blood sooner, and I'll take yours right near climax."

Ann suspected that, based on his choice of when to take and receive, giving must feel better than taking. Unlike so many men she'd been with, she was sure Charles would always abstain if it meant she'd get the better deal.

She leaned down over his body, her bare chest on his. Her taut nipples rubbed against his smooth skin, tingling more pleasure into her. She licked up the hot skin on his neck, rested her lips against his pounding pulse, and ripped into him with her teeth.

A strange, primal energy took over her. Her magic rolled up, smelling blood and connecting that with the brutality of ripping through flesh. A thrill went through her as she licked at his life's blood. Green magic wafted around them, her body wanting to change. To let the wild animal within her maul him, to rip and tear.

Breathing deeply, out of control, Ann rose up, her hands pressing down on his shoulders, keeping him pinned to the mattress. The beginning of a growl vibrated in her throat. The magic around her intensified, caught in the odor of blood. Thinking of a fresh kill and of his sex within her.

Mate.

A weight settled on her chest, heavy and intense. Needy. Desire flooded her senses. The need to possess overcame her, manifesting physically. Her animal was taking the lead.

She scratched up his shoulders and bent back to his neck. Her body squeezed his cock as she gyrated, slow and deep. She ripped into his neck a little more, wild and raw. The hot liquid tumbled over her tongue and lit up her senses.

"Holy shit!" Charles jolted, his hands clutching her tighter. His thrusting stopped. His body went still.

Languid in the way of a mountain lion, she moved over him, squeezing his manhood tight as she stroked him with her body. Her fingers entwined in his hair. Her teeth kept contact with his skin, the equivalent of her fangs on his jugular. Her animal held the power. The control.

She sucked down his blood, feeling his magic saturate her. Colors blasted behind her eyes. Her sex tingled in fierce desire.

She moved faster, working roughly at his neck. Wildly. Her hips swung up and back, graceful but deep movements, commanding him.

He still hadn't moved. His breathing became laborious. His hands clutched her so tightly they would leave bruises.

It only heightened her pleasure.

She took one more long draw, hearing his moan deep in his chest before feeling him shudder under her. He'd just orgasmed, but as she licked at the wound in his skin, not slowing, she could feel his cock still maintaining its hardness, not softening in the slightest.

Wildness still in control, in a mating dance now and unable to stop it, she climbed off him, moving beside him on the bed. She got onto all fours, presenting herself. Wanting her mate to take her like she'd just taken him.

Charles rolled to his hands and knees almost immediately,

somehow knowing what she needed. His large hand ran from the bottom of her spine to the top, applying pressure as it did so. Gently he pushed her upper half down.

She resisted, making him use his strength against hers, firing up his primal side and his need to dominate during a mating. The second push was forceful and filled with power, as he took charge.

She moaned as his hard length seared into her. Hands on her hips, he bore down, thrusting into her as he pulled back, consuming her with pleasure. Making her grunt in ecstasy with each hard thrust.

His hand clenched her shoulder before raising her up as he leaned over. He pushed her head to the side and bit, ripping into her neck.

"Ahhh." She sucked in a breath through her teeth, excitement coursing through her veins with this large male taking her roughly.

He sucked in. The pull at her neck reached all the way to her sex. Bliss pooled in her core. Erotic pleasure tore through her senses. Raw, uninhibited lust stole her breath.

"Yes," she sighed.

He thrust harder, taking her power and using it perfectly. Holding her tightly, trapping her to his body, she was at his mercy. He drew on her neck and pumped into her, crazy and reckless.

Her ardor rose. Her heart pounded. "Yes, Charles!" she yelled, lost to the exquisite sensations.

As his magic shocked through her system, a hard orgasm tore through her consciousness. Waves of pleasure crashed over her. She trembled and shook with the feelings, overcome.

Charles shook behind her, moaning with his release.

In the aftermath, all they did was breathe for a second.

Hard, ragged breaths. A drop of blood trickled down her throat. Their bodies were slick where they touched.

"Are you okay?" Charles asked into the quiet.

"Very. Are you? I sorta... lost the human side of me for a while."

She could feel him shaking his head. "I have never... That was... There are going to be a lot more of my kind fucking your kind, I'll tell you right now. So hot, Ann. I've never had anything like it. It was like you spoke directly to the part of me that is distinctly not human. More primal than if I was just with one of my kind, too. Just... *wild*. Fuck that was good."

"Can you go again?"

His breath hitched. She felt him deflate a little. "Yeah. If you want. I just... I need some time. And to lay down. But I can get there. Just give me a moment."

Ann laughed and wiggled out of his strong arms. "Just kidding! I'm tired."

"Oh thank fuck." Charles sighed and smoothed the sheets on her side. Apparently, he didn't mind sleeping on a dingy mattress, because he wasn't getting up to remake the bed. "I had some doubts about getting hard again. Couldn't admit that, though."

"Ego?"

"Obviously. You can't call your dick magical if it doesn't work miracles."

Ann laughed again and snuggled into him. She vaguely felt his supreme satisfaction. "How quickly does the link take?"

"I can feel your emotions, so apparently no time at all. Barely there, but that'll get stronger. Now, *shhh*. The light is peeping through the window. I need to sleep before anyone shows up that I might have to kill."

She should've been worried. Or terrified. But all Ann felt as Charles' arm came around her was a profound safety. *Mate.*

CHAPTER EIGHT

Charles woke with a start. Daylight streamed in through the windows, lighting up the whole room. Ann was curled up next to him, her head on his chest, her breath deep and even.

A pulse of pain throbbed through his body.

Someone was there.

Charles yanked his arm out from around Ann and hopped up, running to the window nearest the door.

"Wha—" Ann was standing a moment later, pulling on her clothes. Charles felt fear and wariness through their link. The emotions were soft; it would take longer and a few more blood offerings to establish a potent link, but they were there. And damned if they weren't comforting for reasons he couldn't explain.

Charles glanced out the window. In the driveway stood three large men, all wearing suits. One of them swatting at his chest and arms where small points of pain should be spreading across his skin. He'd activated the spell and the others were watching in confusion, not sure what the problem was.

All three of them were human.

"Ann, get in the bathroom."

"Are they just in the front?" she asked, moving quickly.

"For now, yes. Men in suits, probably come to check on why we're here."

"You're naked by the way."

He didn't bother glancing down. "Won't matter."

As the spell withered away, the man stopped swatting himself. He looked around, confusion plain on his face. He said something to the others, but all Charles could make out was the drum of voices. They lingered for a moment longer, the first man brushing invisible dirt off his front, before they all started up the driveway again.

Charles assessed what was coming his way. They were all large, for humans; about six feet two inches, or six-three. All had broad shoulders and thick chests. Their suits were expensive and pristine, but fit more like sacks over the large bodies bulging with muscle. Each had short hair impossible to grab in a fight, but not military buzz cuts. One had a close-cropped beard.

No, almost assuredly not ex-armed forces. That was a good thing. If Charles took out former military personnel, someone would report it to a higher up who would report it higher still. An official would overreact, and then someone would get bombed. Hopefully, these were just private guards, hired to help their employer keep secrets.

A loud knock sounded at the door. Charles pulled it open, letting his pheromones drift out to entrance the minds of these humans.

The men had one moment of suspicious confusion, probably because of his nudity, before their eyes glazed over. The closest one reached for Charles' dick.

"Oh shit." Charles jogged backward, swatting at the hands. "Sorry. Haven't used this in a long time."

CHARLES

He changed the chemical components that made up the pheromones, something so similar to changing elements for a spell that he wondered why humans couldn't do it. When the new mix seeped into the air around him, the man dropped his hand, eyes still glazed over.

"Who do you work for?" Charles asked, ushering the last man in and closing the door behind him.

"Blake Enterprises," the front man said.

"What is their business?"

The man stared straight ahead with a blank face. "They specialize in pharmaceuticals."

"What are they doing up here?"

"This is their experimentation arm. They use live specimens for the new products."

"So, a lab," Charles clarified.

"Yes."

"And what kinds of things are they experimenting with?"

The man blinked twice. "I don't have access to the experiments."

"What do you do, then?"

"I am the Chief of Security."

"Why are you here?" Charles patted the man down, finding a sidearm in a holster.

"We had notice of a possible security breach. This cabin hasn't been occupied for years. We needed to know who was in here, and why."

"Does the lab experiment on humans?" Charles asked, finding similar guns on the other two.

"No human subjects, no."

"Not even humans that change into animals?"

A light crease formed between the man's eyebrows. "Those aren't humans. Those are strange mutations."

Charles ire rose. "Do you experiment on these strange mutations?"

The man kept his mouth shut. His face started to turn red, something in him trying to suppress the need to answer Charles. Charles put more *oomph* into the pheromones.

"Yes," the man blurted in a grunt, spittle flying out of his mouth. "The scientists want to know what causes that mutation. Nothing like it has been documented before."

"And have those scientists documented their finding?"

The man's face turned a deeper crimson. Obviously this was information he was sworn to protect. Charles had to admit, his effort was valiant.

"As far as I know, the scientists keep detailed records of what they find, but they have not been published. They are gathering information. These animal-people heal quickly, and have superior sight, hearing, smell, and strength. Those abilities might help soldiers. There are a lot of possibilities."

"And possibilities means profits." A sick feeling churned in Charles' gut. He felt Ann's disgust though the link. "How many do you have?"

"There are more than two dozen alive."

"Alive?" Charles shifted, pushing down a surge of rage. "All from this area?"

"Only a half-dozen or so came from this area. Most have been captured from areas surrounding our other facilities. When we need new blood, we put the traps in effect. Our methods of capture are unique and genius."

"Genius. No doubt." Charles unclenched his fists, willing calm. "And do you keep these specimens in your other facilities?"

"Absolutely not. Only a privileged few are aware of the existence of these creatures."

"Do the idiots standing behind you know all of this?"

"Most of it, yes. The head guards in this facility need to know of the existence of these creatures to make sure there are no escapes. The creatures have the cunning of humans."

"Because they *are* humans, you fucking disgrace." Charles took a deep breath. "And what happens when someone that doesn't know these are *creatures* empties a trap and finds a person? How do you keep them quiet?"

"That doesn't happen. A special serum forces them to change into an animal."

"And this serum... how do you administer it?"

"Like a gas, it is airborne. It acts like a poison, but instead of killing, it forces change."

"Is that what lures them to the traps?"

"Our luring agent is also an airborne serum, pumped out in large doses. It creates confusion and disorientation. Only the creatures can smell it—I do not know why. Something to do with their genetic makeup. Once the trap is triggered, the other serum is released, though we are having a shortage. We've picked up a lot more of the creatures in the last few weeks. I've heard that the serum is expensive to make."

"I bet. You have to cage people and extract... whatever to make it." Charles looked at his feet. "Well, what I should do is kill you. That's what I should do. You deserve it. But if I kill you, I lose a *lot* of valuable information. So what I'm going to do is have you draw out a map for me. Very detailed so the Boss and Tim can make plans. Then I'm going to make you fuck each other, because big, macho men like you are generally homophobic, and it'll screw with your heads. That'll be my little fuck you. *Then,* I'll let you wake up out of this stupor, preferably with a dick in your ass, and send you back to work, to report. Once we free the shifters, *then* I'll kill you. Or Tim will. Or one of the captives."

The men just stood, blinking at the wall.

Shoulders tight with what was going on up on that hilltop, Charles went to his bag and took out some maps. He placed them on the table, rage simmering deeply inside of him.

"Come over here and give me all the necessary security information."

As the man robotically walked over, Charles said, "Just to clarify, *all* the shifters are in this facility?"

"Yes."

Charles pushed the man into a seat. He handed over a pen. "Do you have any scientists outside of this facility that know about the... creatures?"

"Not that I am aware of, but I couldn't be sure."

"So if this whole place blows up, what will happen?"

A crease formed between the man's eyebrows again. "I really couldn't say."

Charles nodded, because he expected that much, and gave instructions.

∽

Ann sat in the bathroom, fear, unease and rage burning through her. She experienced very similar feelings in Charles. And while she could've left the bathroom, as Charles had the men firmly in hand, she didn't trust herself not to lose sight of the goal and kill them all right where they stood.

She wondered what kind of experimentation they were doing. And how. To get the hormones and whatever else they needed for the serums, more than a few people had probably died.

This was the kind of thing Tim always tried to protect his people from. Fighting with each other was stupid. It was pointless. Fighting with Stefan's people was just as bad. *This,* right here, was the real danger; these were the real enemies. Scientists trying to answer questions were some of the scariest people alive. Even worse? Greedy executives looking at a bottom line with curious scientists under their thumb.

And here they had both. Scientists to investigate, and

executives to sell what the scientists found. They were no better than human traffickers.

Ann stood in a rush of anger and glanced out the window, wanting to get the hell away from this place. At least until she was allowed to go in and blow it all up.

Movement caught her eye. Thirty feet out, about twenty feet beyond Charles' spells, an unusually large coyote looked right at her.

A thrill went through her.

It was a shifter.

"Charles!"

Its ear twitched, hearing her. It didn't move, though, just continued to stare.

"Yeah?" Charles pushed into the small bathroom, right behind her. He saw what she did right away.

"It's a shifter." Ann raised her hand to point.

As soon as Charles appeared, though, the animal took off, scampering through the trees and brush.

"Has to be the one from the other night. Same size and color." Charles stepped back, turning to peer in the main room.

"Do you think he's with them?"

"I don't see how he couldn't be, or he would get trapped." Charles put his hands on his hips. "But I don't see how he could be, with the way these idiots were talking. Doesn't make sense."

"How much longer with those guards?" Ann asked, tightness squeezing her throat.

Charles' eyes softened. He stroked the side of her face. "We'll kill 'em all, don't worry."

"I know. How much longer?"

A grin tweaked his mouth. "Jesus. Impatient much? Want to jump me again? Because I'd be up for it. Magic dick is back in the zone."

"If there was an Olympic sport for thinking about sex, you'd win. Hands down. Gold medal. You'd beat out even boys in puberty."

"Beat out. Like masturbate. Ha! Yeah, I'd win. I can marathon masturbate when I'm bored."

"Oh my God." Ann threw up her hands. "How. Much. *Longer?*"

Charles glanced back into the main room. "These guys are hard-headed, but dense. It takes very little in the way of pheromones to keep them complacent once you've got them on the hook." He walked back into the room, his perfect butt grabbing Ann's attention. Her core started to burn, wanting to touch him.

"The link gives you away, horny!" Charles laughed as he looked down at the table where the guard was working at the map. "Not long now. He's almost done."

Ann's face burned as she went back to the window, looking for that shifter.

"I can feel your embarrassment," Charles called. "You are going to *hate* this link."

"Already do," she muttered, trying to shut out his delight filtering through the link.

It took another ten minutes for the map to be finished. Charles snapped off a few pictures and texted them to Jameson, Stefan, and Tim. After that, he led the guards outside to stage an elaborate setup Sasha would probably not approve of. When he finally came back, his face was grim and his emotions were wary and frustrated.

"What's the matter?" Ann asked, zipping up her duffle bag.

"We need to grab a few pictures of the front entrance and the side fence. Jameson and Tim both want visuals."

"But why? We have everything mapped out. We even have the codes to get into the main gate."

Charles started packing up before *finally* putting on his clothes. She didn't mind nudity—not many shifters did—but the man was distracting at best. She couldn't keep her eyes off certain parts of his body.

"The guard didn't have exact measurements. Jameson and Tim both want distances."

Ann blew out a breath. "Fine. Should we do it now?"

Charles looked out the window. The light was dwindling into the harshness of late afternoon. "Let's give those guards a couple hours to... sort themselves out and head back to their offices. Some humans can fight through the falseness of pheromones, which becomes ten times easier if they see something to jog their memory."

A restless unease filled Ann. As Charles took out his knitting, she got to work straightening the cabin and making some food, anything to keep busy. They'd be going back into danger, if only for a little while. Anywhere near that facility was a bad place to be.

CHAPTER NINE

"Okay, just stay behind me. This is no time to play hero." Charles pinned Ann with a hard stare he'd learned from the Boss. Ordinarily, she would've scowled really hard and made some cutting remark, but this time all she did was stare up at him with hazy eyes.

They were no more than fifty yards from the front of the facility as the darkness consumed the last of the day. According to Ann, the smell of the sweet serum was powerful, overcoming her senses and muddling her thoughts. Her eyes were a little clearer tonight than they had been last night though. The effect on her wasn't as strong. Either his blood and magic was giving her a buffer, or she was getting used to it and able to fight the effects.

They wouldn't be there long enough to figure out which it was.

Charles checked the expensive camera hanging around his neck. It was set to night vision so as not to make a flash. He also had his phone, but still no service. He squinted into the light filtering through the trees from powerful lamps at the front gates.

A paved road to his right saw a car passing every ten minutes or so, no doubt employees heading home for the night. This was the perfect time to move closer and get what he needed. The hustle and mass exodus, together with guard shift changes, would be keeping everyone preoccupied.

"Okay." Charles took another breath and brought Ann in close, hugging her tight. He felt a soft warmth seep through the link, one of love and trust. His heart swelled and his breath grew heavy, never really understanding the depths of her affection until he had been able to get past all her snarky defenses and *felt* them.

"Just stay with me, okay?" he whispered as he laid his cheek on the top of her head. "You'll be fine."

He felt her nod into his chest.

"Okay," he said again, preparing. He let the hard viciousness of battle chase away the soft sentiment from having her close. With the possible danger ahead of them came a clarity to his thoughts and senses. He was ready to protect what was his at all costs. "Let's do this."

He took her hand as he started walking, tugging her so she'd walk *directly* behind him. If there was a trap, he wanted to be the one to fall into it. When he was sure she would comply, he let go, watching his steps and scanning for any human tracks.

They made their way through the trees easily. Light now littered the ground, blaring through the branches and lighting the road a few feet to their right. More cars streamed slowly by, the drivers staring straight ahead. Not one person looked in Charles' direction.

Charles crept to the tree line and hunkered down, reaching behind him and grabbing Ann's shirt, pulling her down beside him. She blinked ahead groggily, shook her head, formed a scowl, and then lost her focus again. She was fighting it, but like any drug, whatever she was ingesting was winning.

Ignoring the raging fear and unease he felt through their link, the effects of her fighting what was happening to her, Charles started snapping pictures of the fence and what lay beyond.

The front of the building had a guard box with two guards in it, checking ID's visually as well as scanning the badges through a machine. And that was to leave. Charles was sure that security would be at least as tight to enter as well. A parking lot inside the gates still held at least two dozen cars.

The main entrance to the facility had another keypad beside two large glass doors. Light shone down on the entrance. Cameras dotted both the walkway and the doors, covering every angle.

It would be tough for a human without magic to get in here. It would be almost impossible for a shifter.

Charles grabbed Ann's upper arm and lifted as he stood, pulling her up beside him. These people were obviously protecting a great secret. It was great news, because outside of this facility, Charles bet not many people would know about it. All this security, in a remote location, meant the big powers probably didn't even trust their employees.

The better news was that for all they thought they knew, and all their intelligence, they were still just humans. Humans without access to their magic. They didn't know what *else* lurked in the night. They didn't know about people like Sasha or Paulie.

They didn't know what kind of retaliation they were inviting by capturing shifters,

Charles tugged Ann closer to the gate, hating how much she stumbled. Hating what that airborne drug was doing to her.

He crouched again at the corner of the road and the tree

line, pulling Ann down behind him. He snapped off a bunch of pictures of the guards and the cars, of the entrance, and things he didn't even think were relevant. Too much information was better than not enough. He then did the same with his phone, just in case, focusing on space and possible points of entry. Anything they couldn't see had already been written down and pointed out by the guard Charles had interviewed.

They had what they needed.

"Let's go." Charles pulled Ann up again, like a ragdoll, and backed away from the road. When the trees obscured them, Charles turned and glanced down at Ann.

She stood loose and limp, staring at nothing. Her battle to fight the confusion had failed. She stumbled blindly, with no clue of what lay around her. Even the emotions coming through the link were lacked any real clarity.

Charles took Ann's hand and pulled her behind, towing her. He noticed a notch in a tree as they passed, a newish slash cutting the bark. He stopped for a moment to take a picture, seeing a pulley at the top with a cable threaded through.

The trap hadn't been sprung.

His brows furrowed as he continued on, wondering why. Perhaps it hadn't been reset?

Ten feet away he found another slash with the same setup. He took pictures of that, too, the makeup of the trap slightly different, and the gash in the side of the tree to anchor the cable much older.

It didn't spring, either.

"I don't like this," he mumbled to himself.

"What?" Ann asked quietly.

He glanced at her, seeing her eyes less hooded and the dullness less apparent. "You better?"

"It's clearing a little."

Charles pointed to the tree with the older scar before moving on. "These traps aren't springing. I don't know why."

"Maybe they just haven't been reset..."

Charles grinned as they kept moving. "That's what I was thinking. But why not?"

An area cleared of mulch underfoot opened up in front of them, the forest floor looking like it had been swept recently. Only new pine needles and a pinecone littered the area. He took a few pictures, before moving on.

"I wonder what that was for," Ann mumbled.

Charles glanced back, and saw that she was checking out the area like he had, and slowed. She shook her head and walked on, about seven feet behind him. He started again as she did, when a sound like a spring attached to a rocket blasted out. He jumped and spun in time to see two nets, one from each side of Ann, wrap around her body.

A thrill of fear went through him, echoed in their link, as he stepped toward her. The ground opened up beneath her feet, a door swinging downward. She fell with a scream, struggling with the netting wrapped around her.

Charles skidded to a halt at the mouth of the hole, looking down into a black pit at least fifteen feet deep.

"Noooo!" Ann said through clenched teeth, struggling with the net. Her body was changing, though. Green enveloped her.

The other serum was active.

"Shit." A list of spells ran through Charles' head, but nothing would help with this. Nothing would hold that door open if it decided to close.

These people were about to find out what really went bump in the night...

As Charles prepared to jump down, a metal grate slid across the opening, cutting him off.

"No!" he yelled, bending to his knees to rip at that grate.

"Get help, Charles," Ann said through painful grunts. "Don't stay. Get help. Get Sasha."

"I won't leave you here, Ann!" Charles answered through clenched teeth.

"Get hrrrrp." Her face changed, her jaw lengthening and growing fur, turning into a mountain lion.

Helplessness and desperation raged through Charles as the link, the new link he shouldn't have been comfortable with yet, was dulled into nothing. He couldn't feel her emotions in an animal state, just that she was alive.

"No, Ann," he begged, ripping at the grate with pain welling up in his chest. "Please, no."

The cry of a mountain lion blasted up at him. Gold feline eyes shocked into him from the pit. She stood on all fours, baring her teeth. If he hadn't known better, he'd have said she'd shed all her fear with her human body.

Get help.

He'd do better. He'd get the most vicious, crazy bastards he knew, and he'd come back and blow this whole place to hell.

"Stay alive, baby," he said down to her, his heart ripping out of his chest. "Stay alive. I'll get you out of here, okay? Just hang on."

A feline grunt answered him, those gold eyes cleared of all the haze.

She'd fight. Now that she was in the middle of it, she'd fight. He knew it as well as he knew his own name. She might've been afraid of what might come when she was a human, but in her primal form, she was hell with claws. Intelligent hell with claws. Who held a grudge.

That's my girl.

A heavy door squealed within the pit. Ann turned that way, taking a few steps back.

"We got another one," a mid-range voice said as a door opened a crack. Charles would remember that voice.

"It still trapped in the nets?" There was a man behind the one Charles could see.

"Mostly. It's standing, though. It's acting like those others—no sign of fear."

"Those others gave us trouble, Ralph. Best hit it with the shock first."

"Nah. I got a tranq dart fit for an elephant." The door opened farther, shedding light in the pit.

Charles saw that Ann was in a cage of sorts, metal bars all around her. The top was open, but the grate made it impossible to escape upwards. A lock held a gate closed. The space was about ten feet by ten feet, with the cage taking up most of that.

Charles snapped off pictures with his phone since the light would disrupt the night vision of the camera. He took pictures of Ralph as he raised a stun gun at Ann, firing off the promised tranquilizer dart. She didn't make a sound as it struck her. Instead, she stared at them while remaining in the proud stance of a great cat.

Her back legs wobbled, but she didn't fall. She continued to stand and stare, as if challenging an intruder to her den.

"Shoulda gone down by now." Ralph looked at his gun in confusion.

"Hit it with another. These things are smart. We don't want to take any chances like the last time. Sam can't see out of one eye."

"I know, I know." Ralph dug in his pocket and came out with a package. "Yup. These are the right ones. Should put this creature out for a whole day, minimum. Why didn't it go down...?"

"Hit it with another!"

"I don't want to kill the thing," Ralph spat back. "We wouldn't get our bonus with a dead critter on our hands."

Charles looked at the grate again, wondering if he could get it open. If he could it would be easy to kill those guards and take back Ann.

"I'd rather lose a bonus than lose my life. Hit it with—"

"All right, all right…" A *pop* sounded, drawing Charles' attention back.

Another dart hit Ann's side. She stood firm for a moment, before her legs started to wobble again. She swayed, looking proud before finally falling.

Charles' heart started beating faster. Something was breaking inside of him as he witnessed her taken down right before his eyes. He couldn't help her. He couldn't get down there and save her.

"There it goes…" Ralph stepped toward the cage as Ann fell, giving a weak growl as she did so. "A fighter, this one. Was probably a military guy, like the other group."

"Get the cattle prod, just to be sure," the other guard said.

Charles sucked in the elements, pulling at fire the hardest, mixing it with air. His tattoos swirled with color as he looked down at two dead men. It was Ralph that noticed, looking up in confusion, and then wide eyes.

Charles shed everything about him that could identify with humans. Anything connected with soft-willed compassion, with temperance and peace, he let go. Then, feeling Ann's magic pulsing through him, he boosted his killer instincts. He gave himself over to his primal side as he stared down at the dull blue eyes of Ralph, dead man number one.

"What the—" Ralph cut off before the smell of urine wafted up. Piss puddled around Ralph's feet.

Charles sent down his own cattle prod, shocking Ralph with the spell Sasha had used since day one. The electricity zapped him, throwing him back.

That's when the other guard looked up, dead man number two.

Charles let the shadows crawl around him, shrouding him in darkness. He amped up his presence, seeing the terror in the eyes of his prey.

They would never forget this moment. They'd be haunted by the fear of him until he cut their worthless lives out from under them. Because they knew Ann was a human. That she was a person. They knew all the *creatures* they captured were still people. It was bad enough to treat animals the way they did, but this facility was going a step beyond with human experiments. And the experimentation wasn't even for the greater good of humanity, it was to figure out what made shifters different so the scientists and executives could bottle it up and sell it to the highest bidder.

Rage overcame Charles as he stood, shadows masking him from the human eyes below. He turned and walked away from the woman he loved with his heart ripping out of his chest.

Because he did love her. He'd loved her since the beginning. He knew that now. There was no thought in it. No second-guessing. She was the woman that had always had a tight hold on his heart, he just hadn't been ready to see it.

Well, he was ready now. He just hoped it wasn't too late.

CHAPTER TEN

"Jonas, they've got Ann." Charles sat on the hood of his SUV in front of the cabin. He'd thought about getting farther away in case someone came calling, but immediately decided against it. He *hoped* someone came.

There was a brief pause before Jonas said, "Did you call Tim?"

"No."

"The Boss?"

"Left a message."

"You gonna tear that bitch down?"

"Yes." Charles looked out through the silent darkness. "Shifters are no good to us in this. They have some kind of special serum up here. We need our kind, and humans with magic. I sent info to Jameson but I don't intend to wait until he has a plan."

"I'll leave here in twenty. Don't do anything stupid until I get there."

Charles dropped the phone to his lap, still staring out into the night. Jonas gave him a lot of shit, but that male would drop everything to help a brother-in-arms, and that included Ann. She was one of the group, despite technically being under Tim's authority. They didn't let one of their own get taken without doing everything they could to rescue her. Without retaliating hard and fast.

∼

Half the night later, a Hummer rumbled into the small driveway. Behind it rolled a line of cars. Jonas had brought an arsenal just as Charles had known he would.

The large male got out, his face grim. Paulie stepped out from the passenger side, a handgun sticking out of the front of his pants. He took a quick glance around before he walked up beside Jonas. The sound of car doors opening and closing filled the night, large males and females in leather gathering around, ready to unleash hell.

"The Boss and Sasha are taking care of something for the Council," Jonas said as he looked at the cabin, and then out at the trees. "They'll be here as soon as they're done. I told them you didn't want to wait. Boss said that was fine, he'd run cleanup."

"Yeah, we're going to have to track more than a few scientists and guards down after this. All the daytime employees." Charles jumped off the hood, holding out his hand to shake with Jonas. He did the same to Paulie. "Thanks for coming."

"They don't take one of ours." Paulie spat and shifted, resting his hand on the handle of his gun. "I brought some street guys. They don't do magic or any of that shit, but they know how to fuck shit up. Thought you might need that to destroy whatever lab they got in there."

"Good." Charles went over how the lab caught shifters, and showed pictures of the various entranceways. When he was finishing up, another car rolled up the road, parking behind the others. After the lights shut off, another male in battle leathers made his way up.

"Jameson," Charles said with a surge of gratitude. Besides the Boss, Jameson was the best leader in battle. He still hadn't warmed to shifters the way Jonas and the Boss had, so Charles hadn't thought he'd jump the gun on a full-scale attack just to save one particular shifter. "You made it."

Jameson glanced at the cabin before shaking Charles' hand. "Ann's always been cool with me. She's fought beside us, saved our Mage, and kept you in line. She doesn't deserve to be in that place."

"And someday we might be the ones in the lab. Better to show our good will, ay Jameson?" Paulie grinned at him. "You're transparent, bro."

Jameson scowled in response.

"Time's wasting. Let's get in gear," Charles badgered.

"Those traps you talked about—they are shifter specific?" Jameson asked, all business.

"They have to be. I walked right over it. *Right* over it. Ann stopped, I was seven feet away, and it triggered. Somehow they can tell when it's a shifter and when it's not. I have no idea how." Charles shook his head as cold determination washed through him. The emotion didn't stem from him.

"Ann's awake." He let the breath out of his lungs slowly, controlling the mad panic to get to her. "She's... angry and determined."

"Blood link?" Jonas asked casually.

Charles just nodded. Jonas matched the nod. No explanation necessary.

"We'll be walking right through the front gate," Jameson explained, jerking his head toward Jonas' car as he started walking that direction. Everyone else followed him. "I brought tech guys. They'll monitor and cut out any outgoing signal before we engage. Once that's done, and we have what we came for, they'll destroy any evidence."

"We need to burn this whole place to the ground," Charles cut in as they stopped behind Jonas' Hummer. "We can't have someone else getting the data on shifters."

"We will acquire all the data, and then we'll burn the place to the ground. Or maybe blow it up," Jameson explained. "We won't know until they've looked over the facility. I want a day, though. If there is tech here we don't know about or have, I want it. After we've stripped this place of its value, *then* we can tear it down."

"You're the boss." Charles' eyes widened as the Hummer tailgate dropped down, showing the interior. Duffle bags containing weapons, stacked high, stared at Charles. Usually they used swords and daggers, but in this trunk lay guns and explosives of all kinds.

Paulie stepped forward and took a semi-automatic assault rifle off the top. "We're not battling a bunch of magical shit. These are humans protecting some bullshit research. They'll have guns. I am making sure we have bigger guns."

"Can you make us invisible yet?" Jonas asked Paulie, taking a similar gun.

"Sure, if you wanna die. I keep inverting the fucking thing and blowing shit up."

"We don't need it—we can use the darkness to mask us. These humans don't know anything about our kind." Charles took the assault rifle from Paulie as a wave of pain flowed through the link.

"They're hurting her. We gotta go." Charles could hear the panic in his voice. He didn't care.

"Let's get on it." Jameson looked behind him at the assembled warriors. "Get armed. Let's go."

～

CHARLES

Ann clenched her teeth as the knife dragged down her arm. A ruddy-faced guard in a gray uniform grinned in at her. "That hurt little lady?"

"What if I stuck that knife in your eye? Would that hurt?" Ann shot back.

The guard chuckled and stepped back, his gaze drifting down her naked body. They hadn't given her anything to cover herself with when she'd woken up, having naturally changed back into a human. She assumed they would when the scientists returned, since everyone else wore hospital gowns, but it seemed this guard wanted to enjoy the sight of a nude female body.

She ignored it as she looked around, scrutinizing the room. She wanted to map out all possible means of escape.

Large cages lined the wall. Half were filled with people she knew, the other half with strangers. She was one of only three women. The strangers were either wild-eyed and desperate, or dull-eyed and nearly lifeless.

In contrast, her pack-mates sat placidly, watching. Hard eyes in grim faces. Eventually someone in this place would slip up, and when they did, Ann's crew would take advantage of it, no matter how long it took. These scientists were used to dealing with animals. Chimps were smart, sure, but they weren't as smart as humans. That was something the scientists might forget.

Ann felt a dribble of blood crawl down her arm. She looked at the wound, relieved that it wasn't deep.

The room was probably forty feet by fifty feet with high ceilings and sterile, metal surfaces. The far wall had more cages lined up—Ann could barely see the tops. She had no idea if they were occupied. In the middle of the floor were operating and dissecting tables, lab stations, harnesses and holsters, many of which looked like they were for large animals. Medical supplies in plenty lined shelves at the end of the room and hung on walls. At the far end were stations with lab equipment.

"They're supposed to be testing us to see if we feel pain," Roger, the pack-mate in the next cage over, said in a low tone as the guard stood by the far door of the lab, cleaning his knife. "During the day, it's just a needle prick. When the scientists aren't around, though, it's a knife. The day guards are mostly cool, but the night guards are screwed up in the head. They've got problems."

"Do those problems then become our problems?" Ann asked in the same low tone so as not to be overheard.

"No, except for cattle prods and knives. The cages are locked with codes. The guards don't know the codes."

"To protect us from them, or them from us...?" Ann mumbled to herself.

"They're trying to get the woman at the end pregnant." Roger pointed to the furthest of the cages.

Ann tried to remember the woman in the cage when she'd been coming to as they brought her in. Small and docile-looking, the woman was extremely skinny and vapid, having long since given up and now probably just waiting for death.

Ann grimaced as her stomach crawled.

"No, not like that," Roger said, apparently reading her facial expression. "It's clinical. Extracting our sperm, though... isn't."

"So they're using you guys to see if she can get pregnant?"

"Yeah. I think they plan to use human sperm for the other woman, to see if that would work better. They've used our sperm to try and impregnate the types of animals we turn into, too. It's all fucked up. All they have to do is ask us. They pretend we can't talk. And if we *do* talk, we get a shock collar."

"Can't you just take off the collar?"

"There are worse things than shock collars. Just keep your mouth shut."

"But they let you talk when they're gone?"

Roger nodded, picking at his nail. "They know we're human. They *know it*. I can see it in their eyes in flashes. In the next second, though, the humanity shuts off and the gleam of a big brain takes over. We are a puzzle, and the first to solve that puzzle gets a prize. At least, that's what it seems like."

Ann blew out a breath. "Well, I brought Charles. And judging by the simmering rage, he's not going to take it easy when he comes to get us."

Roger looked into her cell with calculating eyes. "Did you do that thing where you can sense each other?"

Ann felt her chin raise in defiance. Some shifters didn't trust Stefan's people, others held a firm prejudice against them. They looked down at Ann for spending time with them. "Yes."

Roger nodded as he looked out into the lab. "Good. Can he find you through it?"

Ann let go of a breath she didn't know she was holding. "I think so. I can get a general sense of his direction. Our link is weak, though. It's new."

"You do it in case you got caught?"

"Partially..."

Roger nodded again. "Smart. And he let you, huh? Charles is a cool guy. Not as crazy as that other one."

"Jonas."

"Yeah. Jonas. And that leader with the human wife—they're even crazier. But I'll tell you what, I'll be glad to see them. They're planning to castrate one of us to see how it alters our personality. They wonder if it'll make us more docile, like it does a dog. They wonder if we won't want sex after. Every time they talk about it with their laptops in front of them, one or more of them glances at me."

"Jesus," Ann whispered, tingles spreading through her body.

"Yeah." Roger swallowed hard. "Jesus is right. They've done sexual experiments, too. Put porn on in front of us to see if it'll get us hard, then put on animals, seeing if *that* gets us hard. It's screwed up."

"What else?"

Roger let out a big exhale, shaking his head. "On us new guys, not much. We've had CAT scans, just to check our health and whatever I think. Blood taken, pain tests, healing tests, crap like that. But the older crew... I think they've been through the works. Had their brains sliced into, bodies cut open—not good."

Ann's stomach pinched, partly because the type of torture she'd likely be subjected to in here would probably test her limits. Them breaking her was a very real possibility. And if they gave her an exam, they'd probably include a gynecological one. Charles wasn't human, and he wasn't shifter—his sperm would prove both of those things. It would give these scientists something new to obsess over.

She was, quite possibly, endangering all of Charles' kind as well as her own.

CHAPTER ELEVEN

Charles waited impatiently as he focused on Ann's emotions. She went from disgust to wariness often, occasionally irritation, and sometimes frustration. At least there was no more pain. For now.

Jameson stood next to three guys with laptops at the tree line. Even though they were in sight of the guard booth, no one had noticed them or come over to investigate.

Tim and a crew of shifters waited at the bottom of the mountain road, ready to run interference if they had to. Tim had wanted to come along, but after hearing of the traps and serums directed at shifters, he'd seen reason and stood down. Until they knew how those drugs worked, there was nothing they could do to shut them down before the day crew arrived to work.

"You finally gonna mate her, or what?" Paulie asked as he impatiently tapped his gun with his forefinger.

"Nosey." Jonas stared through the trees at the guard booth.

"There are a ton of those shifters trying to get to her,

man," Paulie retorted. "Not to mention humans staring after her every time we're out. A bunch of guys at the Mansion would cut someone to get her knocked up. If Charles doesn't lock it down, she's gone."

"What are you, a bunch of gossiping chicks? Are we going to braid our hair and pick daisies next?" Charles growled in a voice not unlike Jonas'.

"You're the one who knits, man." Paulie huffed out a laugh. "I'm just filling the time."

"Yes, I'm going to lock it down," Charles admitted.

"Freaked out?" Paulie pushed. "Big step."

Jameson turned back toward them. "We're good. We've got a loop running with the surveillance cameras. Not sure what we'll do in the daytime, but we'll figure it out. Hopefully we won't need it by then. Let's do this."

"Thank fuck," Charles breathed as he stepped forward.

"You can admit that shit, man," Paulie grinned, following him. "We've all been there."

"I haven't been there," Jonas argued.

"You don't count. You're cracked." Paulie took out his gun as his tattoos swirled with color.

Jonas snorted, his own tattoos flaring.

"Okay." Jameson waited until members of the Watch had gathered around. Paulie's street thugs were visible behind them, lacking the ability to mask themselves within the shadows. "This is simple. We walk right through the front door. We don't want to kill everyone—there will be innocents in there. They are just doing their job."

"They're all just doing their job..." Charles said.

"Cleaning floors and shit, he means," Paulie explained. "Not involved in experimentation."

"Security can go down with the ship," Jameson continued. "Keep the scientists alive, if there are any. We need to find out how much they know. I have one group going to the security station, another staying out here to patrol, and a third to rescue those who have been taken. Charles, obviously you'll rescue the taken. Jonas, you're under his command. I'll lead the group to security. Paulie, set your men patrolling out here. I've assigned you some excellent pheromone workers in case any personnel show up to start their day. Daylight is in no more than a couple of hours, so we haven't much time. Worst case, knock people out and put them out of the way to be dealt with later. Many will lose their memories and find themselves relocated—those will be people with no knowledge of shifters or us. Everyone on the same page?"

Movement and nods answered his question. Charles clutched his gun, feeling waves of disgust from Ann, followed by aggression. Someone was pissing her off.

"Let's go." Jameson turned and started to jog. Charles and Jonas followed, side by side. Paulie hung back, probably to get in line with his crew.

When they reached the road, Jameson slowed to a fast walk, his gun out. Charles and Jonas spread out to the sides of him, guns in hands. They walked up the center of the road, straight to the guard booth.

One guard sat at the window, looking out with a dull expression. His eyes slid back and forth over Charles and crew, but failed to focus on them. They were right in front of him, but he still didn't see.

"I'd forgotten how blind humans without magic can be," Jonas said as they came within five feet of the booth.

The guard's eyes snagged on Jameson for a moment before moving off. A crease worked between his eyebrows as his gaze snapped back, settling on Jonas. His head tilted, as if seeing something he wasn't sure of.

Jameson passed right by the booth, without bothering to stop. The guard turned in confusion, watching.

Charles stepped up to the opening as the guard's gaze

found him next. His brows crinkled a little more. "Hello?" The guard's voice came out sounding just as confused as his expression.

Charles reached in and grabbed the man by the front of the shirt. He ripped down, slamming the male's face against the counter. His nose cracked. The man groaned, grabbing his face. Charles let go, moving away when the man slid to the floor.

Paulie could take it from there.

Jameson's crew assembled at the front door, then went in first, magic wrapping around them, keeping them hidden in the shadowed corridors of the sleepy facility. Charles paused at the doors, giving Jameson a few minutes. It'd be easier if the guards didn't know Charles was coming.

After five minutes, Charles nodded at Jonas before sweeping his gaze to the dozen behind them. "Let's go."

They strode along the corridor, guns ready, magic swirling around them. At the first door they found a man in a gray uniform slumped on the ground, his walkie-talkie gone.

Charles checked the map, moving ahead. Gunfire broke out in another part of the facility. Charles paused, his own gun raised.

Pop. Pop. Pop.

"Jameson's crew," Jonas whispered, braced against the wall, looking down the corridor.

Charles started moving again, passing a corridor leading off to the right before reaching one to the left. He turned, ducking back when he saw a man running toward them.

A loud bang sounded. Something hit the wall close to Charles' chest. Paint and plaster sprayed up in a white mist.

"Too bad magic isn't bulletproof," Charles mumbled, ducking out and spraying the corridor with bullets. The man dived toward the ground. Too late. Two red splatters erupted on his chest. He made an "ugh" sound before his body crumpled to the floor.

"All clear," Charles called as he jogged into the corridor, the others following behind.

"You need to stop watching so many movies," Jonas said.

"You're just jealous you don't know the correct lingo for these situations."

Charles glanced at the hand-drawn map, ignoring the many doors that lined the sides of the hallways. As he passed the next corridor, someone yelled up, "Got a shifter back here!"

Surprised, Charles stopped and looked back. One of his guys was standing in the middle of the hallway, looking down a corridor branching off to the right. Charles jogged back and followed his gaze, seeing a large coyote standing in the center of the hallway, facing them. It didn't move. Just stared.

"How'd you know it was a shifter?" Charles asked, pointing his gun.

"Too big not to be. Besides, what would a real coyote be doing in here...?"

To the shifter that had been plaguing him and Ann this whole trip, Charles called, "You better have a damn good reason to turn on your kind, or you'll be dead in the next ten minutes."

A green-red magical mist rose around the coyote like smoke before starting to pop and sizzle. Fur and canine parts morphed into that of a skinny, naked male squatting on the shiny, white floor.

"I ain't never seen a shifter use colors like that to change." Jonas shifted his gun. "And usually their magic doesn't pop and sizzle. This one of those they've been experimenting on?"

"I don't belong to this lab," the quivering man said in a weak voice. He stood, not at all concerned about his nudity, much like all the shifters Charles had met so far. "You need my help."

"You've been hanging around my cabin, you've avoided all the shifter traps, and now you're actually in the lab. Do you expect me to believe you don't belong here?" Charles asked.

"Their drugs don't work on me. Not enough to get me trapped, anyway." The shifter raised his hands above his head, showing he wasn't armed. Not that there was any doubt since he'd just changed from a coyote. Hard to hold a gun without thumbs.

"Why not? And hurry up, because time's wasting."

"My mom was a shifter, but my dad was like you. I'm half and half. I can smell their drugs, but they're vague. Weak. I get a little fuzzy, but not enough to blackout or lose the ability to walk in a straight line. And I can do a little magic, after a fashion."

"Ho-ly shit," someone said behind Charles.

"And you thought Paulie was unique," Jonas said to Charles.

"How'd you get in here?" Charles asked the man, not sure what to do with that information. Or if he should believe it.

"I dug a hole under the fence when they were first putting it up. Since their drugs don't work, I can come and go as I please. The local dogs don't bother me when I'm in coyote form. I had to fight for that privilege, but a shock of magic can really go a long way with a dog."

"What are you doing around here?" Jonas asked in a gruff voice. "Why would you want to come and go if you could get taken at any time?"

"I've followed this lab. They were in New Mexico first. I followed them here. I know what they're doing. In the old place, I could get people out. Not many, and not often, but occasionally they slipped up. Here, though, I don't have the resources. They have surveillance everywhere. High-tech stuff. I know where things are, and I know the codes to free people, but I haven't been able to do anything with it. Last time I tried I got shot at. They think I'm a real coyote since I'm not affected by their traps. I've been in the corridors before—I can mask myself in the shadows like you guys can. But I haven't been able to get past the secondary security."

"Why give up your life to try?" Charles asked, feeling the urgency to get going. If this guy was legit, they could really use his help. If not, they were wasting valuable time.

"My wife is here! They packed her up to move her before I could get her out. I haven't seen them haul her body out to incinerate it, so I know she's still in here somewhere."

Charles looked at Jonas, uncertain. Jonas shrugged. "He's got funky magic, he looks half-starved, I can easily kill him if he steps out of line, and this whole place knows we're here, anyway. Might as well go all in."

Charles turned back to the shifter. "Fine. How can you help?"

"This way is faster. I know the three codes to the cells—I found them in one of the scientist's offices. But I need help getting past the second-tier security."

Charles started walking toward the guy. As he neared, he saw the haunted desperation in his eyes. He smelled as though he hadn't showered in a while and his hair was matted and sticking out at all angles.

"What's this second-tier security like?" Charles asked. "The guard didn't say anything about it."

"At night there is a guard or two at each entrance to the lab where they keep the shifters. Those guards are armed with guns, and they have a panic-button that connects with the main security office. The doors are monitored with cameras on the outside. I don't know about the inside. I tried to slip through when one of the guards wandered away for a moment and someone was at the door within one minute. They started a man-hunt. I was almost caught. They are always watching."

"Not now. Now they're dead," Jonas said.

The shifter walked quickly, turning to the left down a corridor. They passed a dead guard bleeding on the floor. The shifter didn't seem to notice even though he had to step over the body.

Another blast of gunfire sounded in the distance. It was impossible to tell if it was outside or in another part of the facility.

"Where've you been staying?" someone asked from the back.

"Outside, mostly, in my shifter form. When it rained I stayed in one of the cabins around here." The shifter led them around another turn. An empty corridor with shining floors and white walls greeted them. The place was like an asylum. "I eat in coyote form, mostly. I've gone wild in that way."

"Don't eat much, by the look of it," Jonas reflected.

"No." The shifter slowed as they neared the end of the corridor. His body started to shake as he pointed toward the adjoining corridor. "The guards are stationed halfway down in front of a double door without windows. They have guns. One of the night guards notices me. My shadow-magic doesn't seem to work on him. He is off on the weekends, but he should be standing out there now."

"Has magic," Jonas grunted. He looked at the shifter. "He know what's behind those doors?"

"Yes. He antagonizes them. Hurts them and makes fun of them..." The shifter's whole body started to tremble, the look of a broken man.

Charles felt a pierce through his heart. If Ann had been

captured, and Charles knew what was happening to her with no way to save her, he'd probably end up looking exactly like this man. He would follow her around, too. He wouldn't give up on her, and he wouldn't leave her. He'd have the same dismal existence, hoping that someday he could free her and get his love back. To get his life back.

"Well, then. Looks like this guard is about to die." Charles stepped around the corner cloaked in rage and darkness, his magic blasting through his body, spells at the ready. They were nasty spells, too—way worse than being shot.

The guard in question, already standing with a tight grip on his gun, nervous with darting eyes, swung the handgun toward Charles.

Charles already had his assault rifle aimed in his direction. He squeezed the trigger. Bullets sprayed in front of him, piercing the wall, door, and then flesh. The guard jerked back as bullets pounded into him, falling against the wall. His gun clattered to the floor.

The other guard fumbled with his gun. Too late. Bullets battered him next, thumping into his chest and then the wall next to him. Charles wasn't the greatest shot, but with a gun like this, it did not matter in the least.

"Should we throw a grenade just to see it go boom?" Jonas asked with a straight face.

Charles grinned, shooting down the hallway for no other reason than the delight of it. "I wanted to hit him with magic. Too bad he reacted so quickly."

"I like using guns. They're easier than swords." Jonas unloaded a round down the hallway. "Louder, though. They bring cops."

"Shoot your guns for fun after we free my wife, please," the shifter said as he retrieved a key from the guard.

"They have silencers..." Charles let the comment drift away as the door opened. He pushed through, ready for another guard or two. All he saw, though, was a large room with a row of cages on each side. In the center of the room metal gleamed, counter tops and instruments shining even in the dim light. In the first cage, naked and holding the bars with a white-knuckled grip and a relieved smile stood Ann.

"Hi," she said in a gush.

The shifter ran forward, past all the cages, to the cage at the end. Dazed eyes looked up from a broken female hunched inside. Half her head had been shaved and an angry scar puckered her scalp. She blinked as the male's hands reached into her, touching her shoulder.

"Jason?" the woman said in a scratchy, damaged voice.

Charles' heart sank as the male started to cry.

Charles crossed to Ann's cage, reaching through to clasp her hand. Electricity coursed through the contact as his heart surged, mirroring what he felt through the link. He looked down at the keypad as Jonas walked past him, checking the person in each cage, making his way to the door at the other end of the room.

They all heard a loud *boom,* the door being kicked open, before Jonas shouted, "Surprise, fuckers!" Rapid gunfire echoed through the room.

"I need the code!" Charles shouted at the shifter.

"Try 6-5-7-2."

Charles inputted the numbers. A small red light accompanied a *beep*. "Wrong one."

The furthest cage swung open as the shifter—Jason—yelled through sobs, "Try 3-2-9-0."

Charles inputted the numbers. Another *beep* sounded, this time accompanied with a little green light. Metal clicked. The door popped open.

Charles ripped the cage door open and grabbed Ann around the middle, pulling her toward him. He wrapped his arms around her, crushing her to his chest before putting his hands on her cheeks and kissing her sweet lips.

"Be my mate, Ann," Charles heard himself saying, everything else blocked out by the joy of touching her again. Of holding her. Of knowing she was safe. "I'll do whatever you want. Live in a suburb, raise a French poodle named Buttercup, have a litter of fuzzy babies, only play with your breasts. Anything."

"How about taking me on a date?" she asked with tears in her eyes.

"Only if I get a happy ending."

"God, you're a jerk."

He hugged her again, rocking back and forth, so damn happy to have her back.

"We're not done yet, kids. We still gotta get out of here with a bunch of mongrels." Jonas passed by the other way as shifters were helped out of their cages.

"And here I thought he'd be happy to see me." Ann scoffed with a smile.

˜

Ann changed into her animal form, as did the others; faster and more agile that way since they had no guns or clothes.

They headed out the way Charles had come in, stepping over two guards lying dead on the ground. Not one person flinched, but a couple of the shifters who'd been in the lab for a long time gave them a bite as they passed by. If they'd been in human form, it would've been a kick.

The group jogged down the corridor, the coyote that had hung around the cabin leading. The woman from the last cell, limping and missing clumps of fur, ran right next to him.

Gunfire sounded in echoes, ricocheting along the walls.

"We're probably going to run right into that," Charles muttered.

"Can't we go out the side?" Jonas asked.

"No. They have that gas around the side. It's been constant since Ann and I've been here. We should stick to the road with all the shifters or they'll just end up in traps again."

Another blast of gunfire, much louder now, had them slowing down. The coyote trotted to the side of the wall and stopped at the corner, looking back. Charles crept up beside him and peeked around the corner. "Jameson!"

"Come on," Ann heard.

Charles stepped to one side and waved everyone on, winking at Ann as she passed. She hated that she couldn't feel him when she was a shifter.

At the end of that corridor they found Jameson and seven others, all with guns.

"What's up?" Charles asked, stopping near Jameson.

"Silent alarm." Jameson glanced at the shifters, nodding at Ann. "Good to have you guys."

Ann gave a feline huff in acknowledgment.

"I like when she's an animal. It's quieter," Jonas said.

"She's not deaf, bro. You'll pay for all these comments." Charles winked at Ann again. His grin melted off his face as he looked at Jameson. "The cops showed up?"

"No, actually." A single shot fired from the enemy, hitting the far corner. "It looks like a private security company. I suspect this crowd wouldn't want the cops poking their noses into what they have going on in here."

"Explaining human experimentation might get dicey." Charles shook his head. "Where's Paulie?"

"These guys came in the side. He's probably dealing with his own problems in the front." Jameson looked back down the corridor, obviously thinking of other ways they could go around this.

"Fuck it. Let's get the ball rolling." Jonas stepped toward the corner, flush to the wall. He spun into the corridor and lit them up, spraying bullets as he moved his gun back and forth. Charles stepped up beside him and threw something, pulling Jonas back as something clanged on the floor down the hallway.

"Fire in the hole!" Charles yelled, pushing everyone back.

Yelling erupted down the corridor before a huge blast rocked the building. A couple ceiling tiles dropped down around them. A crack formed in the wall.

"Nice." Jonas gave a rare smile.

Shaking his head, Jameson looked around the corner quickly before pulling back. He looked around again, leaving his head out in the open a little longer. He stepped out slowly.

"That was a moan," Jameson said, jogging out of sight. Charles took off with him.

Ann ran around, catching up with Charles quickly. Down the way a jagged hole gaped within the wall, showing a dark room with various silver vats inside. Debris littered the ground. Around a fractured corner lay two men.

"Let's go. Careful, though. We don't know where they are now." Jameson started at a jog, not taking his own advice. He ran down the corridor, staying close to the wall. More gunshots sounded, but they were distant.

As Jameson turned left at the next corridor, the coyote barked. He stopped in the middle, stepping the other way while looking back. Charles stopped next to him, looking at Jameson. "This guy has been around here for a while. He knows where he's going."

Jameson took out his map, tracing a path with his finger. His hard gaze hit Charles. "You sure?"

"You think he wants to get caught in this place?" Charles beckoned Jameson forward. "Let's go."

They followed the coyote through twists and turns, wandering through areas that must've been staff quarters and offices, including a break room and kitchen. They didn't see a soul: most of the lights had been off, only turning on when the group ran through. The way was obviously longer, but ten times safer, which meant it was faster. The coyote just wanted to get out of there. Ann didn't blame him.

The route led them back down a main drag, this hallway wider than the others, with staff pictures on the walls and cheery signs welcoming all employees. Bodies littered the ground, all in gray or black uniforms, many large, and all bleeding.

Jameson, retaking the lead with Charles and Jonas, slowed down, tiptoeing over the bodies still gripping their guns. A blast sounded somewhere outside, shaking the glass of the sliding glass door twenty feet in front of them. Another sounded. Red sparklers floated by the door before popping with a series of bangs.

"Sasha," Charles said with a sigh.

Another loud bang sounded to their right. Gunfire.

Jameson staggered left, his body turning and firing his gun even as he slumped back against the wall.

Faster than thought, Charles had something near his mouth before he was throwing. Jonas fired his gun as the object flew down an intersecting corridor.

"Fire in the hole," Charles shouted, grabbing Jameson and throwing him over his shoulder lurching out of harm's way.

A huge blast shook the building. One of the glass doors shattered.

"Clear the way. We need to get him out of here!" Charles yelled at the other Watch members.

Three people stepped into the intersecting area of the

corridors, guns ready. Ann loped ahead, only to hear Charles say, "Not you, Ann. Shifters need to stay back. We don't know what's going on with the gas outside."

The three must've found emptiness, because one stayed there while the other two ran out through the main doors.

With green-red mist, sizzling and popping, the coyote turned into a skinny man, face grim. He stepped up to Charles quickly. "Put him down. I was a nurse in the emergency ward. I can help."

Jonas and Charles worked together to get Jameson to the ground as carefully as they possibly could. A moment later, Stefan was running through the glass door, dressed in leathers with a terrifying look of rage painting his face. Paulie was right behind him, guns out.

"What happened?" Stefan demanded, doing a quick sweep with his dark gaze before bending to Jameson.

"Gunshot. We don't know how bad," Jonas said as he ripped Jameson's shirt down the front and gently pulled it back. On the left side of his torso blood oozed down his skin.

"Lift him up a little," the skinny man said. "I need to see if there is an exit wound."

"We just need him good enough to get him to the bottom of the mountain," Stefan said in a commanding tone. "Tim brought his medical staff, assuming some of the shifters would need it."

"Some will. But he'll need it more," the man said, nodding with the blood pouring down Jameson's back. "Exit wound, looks clean. There's nothing lodged inside. We need cloth to apply pressure to both wounds to slow the blood before you move him out of here. Hopefully that bullet missed the vital organs. If so, he heals fast enough to get out of harm's way."

Stefan didn't even have to utter the command. Four people stepped up, each strong enough to take him on their own, but working together in order to avoid jarring him.

Jameson's face had gone deathly pale. He grimaced as they moved him, clearly in pain.

"Charles, Jonas, get the shifters out of here." Stefan's hard gaze landed on Ann. He winked. "Glad you made it."

"What's going on outside?" Charles asked, gesturing for Ann and everyone to head toward the door.

"Paulie took care of the security trying to get in through the front. We'll have to alter and hide memories for those who lived. Some came in the side gates, though. Not many of those will be alive by the look of it. I have people on all the exits and Sasha has a concealment spell on the building for now. Once Jameson is patched up..." Stefan moved slightly. His mouth turned into a thin line. He took a deep breath, obviously worried for his friend. "Once he's patched up, he'll want access to this place before we blow it up, or whatever we're going to do. We've started to gather scientists and other personnel now. I understand they don't know about us, just shifters..."

"That's right," Charles answered. "But Ann's got my blood and DNA inside her. They would've found it, and they would've been suspicious. The trail of breadcrumbs was there. If they had more time, who knows what they would've uncovered..."

"The trail of breadcrumbs to both shifters and our kind has always been there." Stefan looked around at the walls, his face grim. "But at least we have some time."

Charles glanced at Ann. "Do you want me to come back after I take them to Tim?"

Stefan glanced at Ann, then back at Charles. "No. Take Ann home. We can wrap it up here."

"Thanks, Boss."

They moved out in a tightly packed horde. Jonas walked in front of those carrying Jameson with Charles walking between Jameson and the shifters. As they stepped out into the daylight, Ann couldn't help a jolt of surprise at the mayhem. Bodies and broken glass littered the entranceway and outside the gates. Cars had been pulled off to the side in defensive positions, men probably using them to hide behind as bullets zinged past. People were seated in clusters, tied up and gagged.

Paulie caught sight of their group and stepped out from beside the guard booth. His gaze snagged on Jameson before he whipped around. "Get some more SUVs or vans up here! We got a few more to transport!"

A couple large men with grim expressions and many tattoos jogged toward the parking lot.

"Gunshot wound?" Paulie asked Jonas as he walked forward.

"Yeah. Sounds like it went right through him, but we gotta stop the blood. You have many casualties?" Jonas looked at the fallen men around them as three vehicles pulled up, all with the uniforms of the enemy guards.

"Some. We've moved them all down the mountain. I hit the guards that showed up pretty hard with magic, not to mention we had bigger weapons. We didn't take many losses compared to their side."

Jonas nodded as the first large van stopped beside them. He turned to help get Jameson loaded up as Charles gestured at the second and third vans. He motioned to the shifters. "Get in. Let's get moving."

It took no time at all to get everyone organized and on the way. Paulie called ahead on his walkie-talkie, making sure the road was clear as they sped down the mountain. At the bottom awaited a well-organized area with tents and water stations. Various shifters were tending to the wounded.

Charles was out as soon as the van stopped, walking ahead quickly to help get Jameson situated. All the shifters climbed out of the car as well, Ann's pack shepherding the strangers toward the tents.

Ann let her magic course through her, changing into her human form. Not worried about nudity, she found Tim striding out of the large tent in the middle of the makeshift camp. When he saw her, his step faltered. He grabbed her roughly and squeezed her into his chest.

"Thank God you're okay." He held her at arm's length and looked deeply into her eyes. "You are okay...?"

"Yes. I think all our guys are good. They'll probably have nightmares, but it could've been worse. We have others with us—the ones who've been in that place a while. They need special handling."

Tim's brows furrowed. He gave a curt nod, a trace of disgust on his features. He was probably imagining what they'd been through. Unfortunately, the reality wouldn't ease his mind. "Without question. We'll get them taken care of."

Ann felt a pulse of possession through the blood link a moment before she heard, "Ann. Ready?"

She stepped away from Tim, turning toward Charles as he strode up. A hard gaze hit Tim as Charles' arm fell around her shoulders. "Everything good?"

"How's Jameson?" Ann asked, trying to hide her pleasure at the unmistakable claim Charles was putting on her. It was something a shifter would've done with his mate if another male was too close.

Tim respectfully took a step back.

Charles' muscles relaxed as he said, "They have him on an IV. He's lost a lot of blood, but they think that's the extent of it. He'll be okay." He took a deep breath before sticking out his hand to Tim. "Thanks for setting this up. You probably saved his life. A lot of lives."

Tim nodded in a matter-of-fact sort of way, his gaze

staying on Charles. "You guys helped us out. This was the least we could do."

"Am I needed?" Ann asked, weariness tugging at her features.

Tim looked at her then. He was all alpha though, hiding any feelings he might still have had for her. He'd always been an awesome guy, and now he was proving it. "No. You've been through hell. Get some rest."

Ann nodded and let Charles lead her away.

EPILOGUE

Ann waited impatiently on Sasha's couch, sipping a glass of wine. It had been two weeks since she'd been freed from the lab. In that time, they'd segregated out the scientists who had experimented on shifters, the executives who knew about it, and everyone else. Those who knew nothing got to go about their lives. The others were pumped for information. After that... Ann had no idea what happened to them. Tim and Stefan were being very tight-lipped about it, and Sasha didn't want to know. She suspected it was probably bad. Ann had to agree.

Not knowing was probably better.

Jameson survived. The bullet had missed all the vital organs, but by the time he got worked on he had nearly bled out. It took him a week to recuperate enough to head to the lab and start handing out orders. He wanted tech looked at, the traps analyzed, and all sorts of things that would make Stefan's clan the most knowledgeable and high-tech in the country, possibly the world.

As far as the press went, though, a strange gas leak caught fire and blew the place up. Sasha rigged a spell to fool the eye into believing that story until they really could blow it up, which would happen as soon as Jameson had everything he wanted.

And here sat Ann, waiting for Charles to pick her up for their first date. She'd seen him every day since the lab, but that was just for sex, cuddling and banter. Tonight was the real thing.

"He keeps asking me to be his mate," Ann said, her sip turning into a gulp.

"That's what you wanted, though, right?" Sasha asked in a calm voice.

"Yes. Obviously. But... he came around awfully fast, you know? It was like—no, no, no, I want to be a slut! Wait, yes, let's get married, have babies, and become Sasha and Stefan."

"You did sex him up pretty good."

"That's just it. If it's just sex, that's bad, because he gets bored easily."

"You also connected on a really deep level, made him feel okay about cuddling, which he really never does, got taken by an enemy... You forced the man to grow up, that's all. Well... mostly grow up. I don't know if he'll ever be mature."

Ann finished her glass of wine, and went for a second. Her nerves were frayed.

"I'm jealous about the date, though," Sasha said, rocking back and forth in her rocking chair. "The number of romance novels and rom-coms he's watched to try and get into yours and my pants... this date is probably going to be way over the top in a good way. Wait—don't you know how he really feels about you? The blood link is solid now, right?"

"Yeah but... I don't know. Maybe he's just temporarily confused..."

"You're just being an idiot girl with low self-esteem. You can feel that he loves you. So he loves you. Trust me, Charles would fake love about as fast as he would fake an orgasm. Not gonna happen."

"He hasn't said it, though."

"Neither have you," Sasha reasoned.

"Because he hasn't…"

"Was I ever this stupid? I don't think I was… No, I'm pretty sure I was never this harebrained."

"You still are when it comes to Stefan."

"Nope. You're wrong." Sasha scratched her belly.

The doorbell rang, sending a nervous shiver through Ann. She smoothed her hair and then her dress, turning to Sasha. "How do I look?"

Sasha rolled her eyes as the front door opened. "For the millionth time, that dress is sexy as hell, I hate you for the glossy hair, nice boobs; you look great…"

Ann took another gulp of her wine as Jonas came into the room.

"What are you doing here?" Ann asked with a scowl.

Jonas huffed and crossed to his favorite recliner. "Came to watch the show."

"What show? He's just picking her up." Sasha stalled in her rocking.

A soft knock sounded before the front door opened. Another wave of nervousness rolled through Ann.

"What's he feeling?" Sasha asked, rocking again. "If he's nervous, you should be worried. It means he's done something wrong and is afraid you're going to kill him."

"He has the link blocked." Ann sat back down, crossed a leg, thought better of it, and crossed her ankles instead.

"Why?" Sasha asked suspiciously.

"I asked him. I knew I'd be nervous and I didn't want him to know I was nervous."

This time Sasha gave her an eye-roll. "Why?"

"Just because. Quit asking questions." Ann looked up as someone appeared in the archway. Her breath caught.

Charles stood with a dozen red roses and a little box, his smoky-gray eyes sparkling as he looked at her. He smiled, walking toward her in the graceful way predators had. His black shirt fit snugly across his large chest and broad shoulders, showing off a little pec that made her mouth water. His handsome face was smooth and clear of stubble. "Do you want me to sit, or should we get away from Jonas? He's a buzzkill."

"Impressive flowers. Trying to make up for a small dick?" Jonas asked, leaning back in the chair.

"What'd you give Emmy?" Charles thought about it for a second. "Oh right, nothing."

"I gave her a baby."

"You *gave* her a baby?" Sasha chimed in. "Is that right? Well how generous of you, Jonas. You had a few moments of pleasure, which she may or may not have shared, and then you gave her nine months of morning sickness, heartburn, peeing herself, and uncomfortable nights, only to ruin her vagina. Well, happy-happy, you gave her a baby. What a great guy..."

"Okie..." Ann got off the couch with a grimace and left her glass on the end table. "That's our cue, Charles."

"Don't leave me here with her..." Jonas begged.

"Why is that, Jonas?" Sasha started again, grumpy and now having someone to take it out on.

"For you," Charles said as they walked toward the door quickly. He nodded toward the flowers, but handed her the box. "I was hoping to leave the flowers here in a vase, but Jonas is just going to stick his foot in it again, so if they die, I'll buy you new ones."

Ann smiled, warmth filling her chest. They stepped outside into the crisp night air. The motion sensor blinked on, showering them in light. Ann took the wrapping off the velvet black box. When she opened it, she sucked in a breath. It was a beautiful diamond necklace, glittering for all it was worth.

"Charles, it's beautiful," she gushed.

"I see you're wearing a necklace, so I won't step around you to put it on."

Ann smiled with the sentiment, handing it back to him so she could remove her cheap costume jewelry. She opened the door to Sasha's house and just threw it in. She'd get it later.

"Okay. All set." Ann took the box back and held it up for Charles. He tucked the flowers under his arm and took the necklace out, crossing behind her to fasten it to her neck. His fingers played lightly over her skin, tickling and giving her goosebumps.

When he stepped back in front of her, he bent and kissed her cheek. "You look beautiful, by the way."

She preened, smoothing her dress before reaching for the flowers.

"Shall we?" he gestured out toward the street where the Boss' Ferrari waited. "If you don't want the sports car, my SUV is parked around the side."

"Let's take your car," Ann said softly, sliding her hand down his muscular arm and entwining her fingers through his.

"Sure. And because this is a date, and I am on my best behavior, I will not point out that the backseat in my ride is way larger than the Ferrari's nonexistent backseat."

"Duly noted." Ann laughed as they walked around the corner to his SUV. Once there, he opened the door for her and let her climb in, helping her up with a hand on her arm.

"You'd almost think I was clumsy..." Ann said with a grin.

"You are. I don't want you falling on your head."

He gave her his beautiful smile, amplifying his handsomeness as he walked around to his side and climbing in. Once they were moving, he reached over and took her hand, threading his fingers between hers.

"This isn't the traditional date you're probably expecting," he said in a soft voice as he drove in the opposite direction of the city. "I'll do that for you next time, if you want. This one is... more original."

"What's traditional?"

"Dinner at a nice restaurant, dessert, then either a movie or dancing. Or a quiet spot with just the two of us listening to the radio softly and talking or just enjoying the night with wine."

"Do you take notes when you watch the romance movies...?" she said, blinking at him.

"They're really all the same," he answered seriously. "You've seen three, you've seen them all. You women don't seem to want much when you're being chased. It's after that that things get complicated, I think. Or maybe Sasha is just bat-shit crazy."

"Both, I think," Ann laughed. "I'm not any better, though."

"Oh, I know. I've known you for long enough now." Charles laughed, light and carefree, as he pulled into the driveway of a well-lit house with an adorable porch swing and large, grassy front yard.

"Whose house is this?" Ann asked in confusion.

Charles winked at her as he turned off the car. He hopped out and came around to her side, helping her down. Still confused, she let him lead her up that front walk to the porch. Once there, he stopped and pulled another black, velvet box out of his pocket.

Facing her, he dropped to one knee.

Her mouth dropped open as he held up the box. Slowly, he opened it. Instead of a ring was a shiny, metal key. "Ann Mallory, will you marry me?"

"Whaaa..." Confusion growing, she reached forward and took the key gingerly.

"I know the standard proposal item is a ring, but you turn into a mountain lion. I thought more jewelry wasn't a great idea," he explained, standing and gently wrapping his hand around hers. He slowly moved her hand toward the front door. "So I figured the next best thing would be a house. It's really a much more practical gift. And if you say yes, I'll live here with you. And if you say no... well, I'll probably spend every night here with you, anyway, because I promised that yours were the only breasts I would play with, so I need to be close. That's a must."

Ann's mouth was still unflatteringly hanging open as Charles helped direct the key to the lock. The deadbolt clicked over. He pushed the door open. "Can I take away the block on the blood link, now?"

She nodded, still stunned mute. As his cover ripped away, pure, raw love poured through the link, filling her up. Turning her chest warm. He took her hand and led her inside, where the floor was covered in rose petals and crystal vases filled with red roses dotting the bare hardwood floor.

He led her to the living room, where a foldout table with a white tablecloth was stationed in front of the empty fireplace. He had her sit down before lighting the candles on the table. "I made dinner, which I burned. So then I had Jessenta make dinner and I brought it over here to keep warm in the oven. So if you wait right here, I'll go grab it."

Charles looked down on her for a moment, before smiling and leaning down for a soft kiss on her cheek. He headed to the kitchen, his butt perfectly sculpted and shown off in his tan slacks. He came back with two plates held in pot holders. After placing them he disappeared again, returning with a basket of bread and a bottle of wine.

She didn't even notice what was on her plate. Or what

type of wine it was. All she could do was stare at Charles, perhaps the most thoughtful and handsome man on the planet. In all his crazy and random humor, and his occasional dim-witted remarks, he was a true, honest, loyal man with a heart of gold. And he was asking to marry her. He was giving up on his desire to screw his way through the Mansion so he could be with her, totally and completely, because that's what she needed from him.

It was more than any man she'd ever been with would do for her. Would do for anyone, she had no doubt.

"There's no furniture," she said stupidly, the love she felt dripping down into her core and settling there with an erotic hum.

His smile and suddenly burning eyes said he felt that through the link. "There's furniture in your bedroom. Not much, and easily replaced if you want something else, but I figured we needed a place to sleep."

"Our bedroom." Her eyes glossed over with unshed tears. "Yes, Charles. Yes, I'll marry you."

He smiled, reaching for her hand. "When do you want to try for a baby? I'd love to have one of my own, the Gods willing."

"Now," she whispered, standing. "Right now."

Dinner forgotten, Charles blew out the candles, stood, and scooped her up. As he carried her upstairs to their bedroom, he said, "Our baby will be way cuter than Jonas'. Emmy's pretty, sure, but you need two parents to be hot for the win."

"And you think you're hot?"

"Obviously. Way hotter than Jonas, at any rate." As Charles crossed the threshold with her squeezed tightly to his chest, he said, "Do shifters have furry babies? I've joked about that, but are we going to have little mountain lions?"

Ann laughed. "That guy Jason was both a shifter and could

work magic. Red level, too. I bet our children will be able to do both."

"But like... do you have cubs, or..."

"We don't change until puberty, dummy. I won't have a litter."

Charles just smiled as he gently put her down. He kissed her softly. "As long as I have you, the rest is just gravy."

_-*-*-*-*-*-*-*-*-*-*-*-_

Thank you for taking the time to read my ebook.

Check out Chosen, book 1 of the Warrior Chronicles:

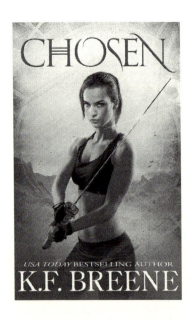

Never miss a new release or sale: http://eepurl.com/F3kmT

Website: Kfbreene.com
Facebook: www.facebook.com/authorKF
Fan and Social Group: https://goo.gl/KAgoNr
Twitter: @KFBreene

Review it. Please support the book and help others by telling them what you liked by reviewing on Amazon or Goodreads or other stores. If you do write a review, please send me an email to let me know (KFBreene@gmail.com) so I can thank you personally! Or visit me at http://www.kfbreene.com.

Lend it! All my books are lending-enabled. Please share with your friends.

Recommend it. If you think someone else might like this book, please help pass the title along to friends, readers' groups, or discussions.

ABOUT THE AUTHOR

K.F. Breene is a USA TODAY BESTSELLING author of the Darkness Series and Warrior Chronicles. She lives in wine country where over every rolling hill, or behind every cow, an evil sorcerer might be plotting his next villainous deed while holding a bottle of wine and brick of cheese. Her husband thinks she's cracked for wandering around, muttering about magic and swords. Her kids are on board with her fantastical imagination, except when the description of the monsters becomes too real.

She'll wait until they're older to tell them that monsters are real, and so is the magic to fight them. She wants them to sleep through the night, after all…

Never miss the next monster! Sign up here!

Join the reader group to chat with her personally: https://goo.gl/KAgoNr

Contact info:
kfbreene.com/
kfbreene@gmail.com

Made in the USA
Las Vegas, NV
13 September 2021